A MOMENT OF MAGIC

A moment of magic could not be compared with the lifetime of loving that Giles seemed to offer. Elfrida decided that she had attached too much importance to the feelings that his brother had evoked too easily. She would marry Giles who would never give her a moment's disquiet and would be a loyal and loving husband. What more could any woman want . . . ?

Books by *Juliet Gray*
in the *Linford Romance Library:*

WHEN FORTUNE SMILES
BID ME LOVE
ALWAYS IS FOR EVER
THE COST OF LOVING
A HEART FOR HEALING
THIS IS MY DESTINY
SWEET REBEL
SHADOW ON A STAR
RAINBOW GOLD
ARROW OF DESIRE
THE CRYSTAL CAGE
A TOUCH OF TENDERNESS
THIS SIDE OF HEAVEN
TOO MANY LOVES
KEY TO THE PAST
LOVE IS A RAINBOW
BRIDE FOR A BENEDICT
HEART OF GLASS

JULIET GRAY

A MOMENT OF MAGIC

Complete and Unabridged

LINFORD
Leicester

First published in Great Britain in 1979

First Linford Edition
published 2001

British Library CIP Data

Gray, Juliet, *1933* –
  A moment of magic.—Large print ed.—
Linford romance library
1. Love stories
2. Large type books
I. Title
823.9'14 [F]

ISBN 0–7089–4571–6

Published by
F. A. Thorpe (Publishing)
Anstey, Leicestershire

Set by Words & Graphics Ltd.
Anstey, Leicestershire
Printed and bound in Great Britain by
T. J. International Ltd., Padstow, Cornwall

This book is printed on acid-free paper

1

Elfrida paused to look about her and then plunged deeper into the copse, an intrepid explorer of the unknown, feeling as adventurous and as deliciously excited as though she were ten instead of twenty-two. It was a lovely afternoon in early summer and she had obeyed her father's request for solitude and taken herself for a ramble across the fields and down the country lanes that bordered the village of Frisby. The cool green depths of the wood had tempted her to stray from the exposed and well-worn path.

Bright sunshine filtering through the tall trees transformed a small clearing into an enchanted glade and Elfrida, delighted, began to make her way through the tangled bracken which surrounded the clearing. Feeling a tug at her dress, she glanced round to find that her skirt was entangled in the thorns of a bramble bush. The frock was old and rather shabby, entirely suited to the afternoon's adventures, a bright splash of yellow that competed with the sunshine amid the shadows. But she took pains to free the material from the thorns without tearing it ... and was so absorbed in the task that she was unaware of being observed until a man's harsh and unmistakably hostile challenge, apparently out of nowhere, startled her so much that she turned swiftly, ripping her dress free with the movement.

He stood in the middle of the clearing, legs apart in an arrogant stance, a rifle held carelessly across his arm. He was tall and powerfully-built, his bronze-coloured hair glinting to gold where the sun struck it, and he might have been remarkably handsome were it not for the angry scowl that touched his grey eyes and the fury that tightened his jawline and caused the pulse to throb at the corner of his mouth.

'Oh . . . You startled me!' Elfrida exclaimed involuntarily, a hand at her breast to still her leaping heart.

His glance raked her from head to foot, taking in the shabby frock, the bare, brown limbs, the tangle of wind-blown hair that tumbled about her slender shoulders in a cascade of thick black curls, the rather elfin features. He observed her youth and disregarded her beauty. His eyes hardened, narrowed. 'You're trespassing,' he repeated curtly.

Her chin had tilted just a fraction before that faintly contemptuous scrutiny. Now she looked back at him with a pride that he merely interpreted as defiance. 'I haven't seen any signs to tell me so,' she said coolly, fiercely resenting his attitude.

'These are private grounds as you very well know, I daresay,' he snapped. 'You and your kind are all alike . . . swarming all over the countryside

3

and taking what you want and caring for nobody!'

There was such hostility in the grey eyes that Elfrida was alarmed. Quite instinctively, she took a step backwards into the brambles, scratching her legs, ready to run like the wind if he should move towards her. She did not care at all for the look in his eyes. 'I'm sorry,' she said.

'You will be if I catch you here again,' he returned grimly. 'Now get along — and tell the rest of your tribe to leave my land by nightfall or face the consequences. You are not welcome here!'

He turned and strode away through the trees, departing as suddenly as he had arrived — and Elfrida stared after him in dismay, realizing that he had mistaken her for one of the gypsies who had halted their caravans in a field on the outskirts of the village only the previous evening. She had passed their camp on her way and smiled a little shyly at those who glanced at her but evoked no response from the instinctively suspicious people.

She was indignant. Then, suddenly aware of her tumbled hair and shabby frock and bare, scratched legs and arms, she supposed she could not blame him but she did wonder why he should regard the gypsies with such evident loathing. It seemed to Elfrida that it had been rather more than the usual distrust of a way of life so alien to the conventional.

Beyond the copse lay the Inskip estates and she did not doubt that he was one of the Inskip brothers. But she had thought that this wood was common land and she had not explored it with any thought of trespassing. She was rather puzzled to know what harm he supposed her to be doing. Still indignant, her face flushed from the encounter with such an aggressive personality, she began to retrace her steps, wondering which Inskip he could be. There were four of them, she knew. Elfrida and her father were newcomers to Frisby but they had already heard a great deal about the family who owned most of the village and much of the surrounding land.

They were the sons of Midas Inskip who had apparently lived up to his name so thoroughly that he was still referred to as Lucky Mid by the villagers although he had been dead for more than ten years. Landowner, member of parliament, local magistrate and church-warden, master of the hunt, philanthropist, loved and revered by all who knew him, Midas Inskip seemed to have been one of those fortunate people who succeed in every aspect of life — everything he touched had apparently turned instantly to gold! Elfrida did not know if his sons had inherited that lucky touch but, recalling the arrogant stamp of one Inskip's features, she felt that it was not only Lucky Mid who had been accustomed to having everything go his way. At least one of his sons expected instant and unprotesting deference to his authority,

Elfrida thought, wishing she had stood her ground and not allowed him to awe her into a meek submission that was totally out of character!

She had been at a disadvantage, of course — not only trespassing but looking every inch the raggle-taggle gipsy he had supposed her to be, she thought wryly, sweeping the tangle of curls from her small face with undeniably grubby and bramble-scratched hands. It was not at all how she had planned her first meeting with an Inskip . . . but if they were all alike then she no longer had the slightest desire to become acquainted with them!

Her father had declared that he did not mean to further a very slight acquaintance with the eldest Inskip as he would be busy with the new book he was writing and would have little time or inclination for the social niceties. And if the Inskips were aware of Owen Hendry's recent arrival in the village they had not betrayed any sign of it or shown any neighbourly interest. Nor, it seemed, were the villagers impressed by her father's name or fame as writer and television personality. Apparently the famous could come and the famous could go but the peaceful tide of life in Frisby would go on its way undisturbed.

Elfrida had fallen in love with the quiet beauty of the village and the surrounding country was much to her taste. She was content to spend a summer in Frisby. It was unlikely that they would remain for the winter although their rented cottage was both comfortable and convenient. Owen Hendry was a restless, impulsive and somewhat eccentric man who was always finding the only place in the world where he could settle — and being disappointed within weeks of their arrival!

As a result, Elfrida was much-travelled and very adaptable. She had lost count of the houses and hotels that had been temporarily home, the schools she had attended, the friends she had made only to lose when her father moved on to fresh fields. She did not share his wanderlust. With all the intensity of youth, she longed for a real home, for roots, for binding and permanent relationships. But she loved her father and it pleased him to keep her with him and until a knight in shining armour galloped up on his white charger to sweep her off to a very permanent castle where all her dreams would come true, Elfrida was happy with the way of life that she knew with her father. In truth they were a pair of gipsies, she thought with a faintly rueful smile — but it had certainly not pleased her to be dismissed as such so carelessly, so contemptuously by an arrogant, over-bearing, totally manner-less stranger!

She was a little surprised to find how far she had ventured into the wood. She had not supposed it so far to the road that would take her back to the village. She came to a halt, looking about her. She could not recall the strikingly odd shape of that tree which must have impressed her if she had passed it earlier . . . and yet she could have sworn that she was accurately retracing her steps. She was far from being lost, of course . . . ridiculous to think it possible in such a small wood! She had simply taken a wrong turning along the way. The copse was quite overgrown at this point. The warmth of the sun seemed unable to penetrate the thick foliage of the trees above her head and she was surprised to discover that she felt quite chilled in her thin frock.

A dog barked in the near distance and she turned towards the sound, remembering the farmhouse she had passed before she reached the wood and the trio of watchful dogs in the yard. A bright patch of sunshine lured her with the hope that it indicated the thinning of the trees and the beginning of open land. She pushed her way through a clump of bushes and unexpectedly found herself at the edge of a small lake in a clearing. She caught her breath at its beauty and instantly stooped to trail her fingers in the cold, clear water. The dog barked again, much nearer this time, and then came bounding out of a thicket towards her. He was a sleek and elegant hound, little more than a playful puppy, and Elfrida was amused when he leaped up to befriend her with a briskly wagging tail and an unmistakable smile in his velvety brown eyes.

'Oh, you beauty!' she exclaimed warmly, laughing softly and responding to the exuberance of his greeting. 'But where do you come from? Have you come to rescue me?'

'Do you need rescuing?'

For the second time, she was startled by the sound of a man's voice when she least expected it. But she instantly realized that she ought to have expected the dog to be accompanied by its owner.

She looked round to find a tall young man leaning against a tree trunk and regarding her with warm friendliness in his smile. The similarity of grey eyes and auburn hair and striking good looks declared his relationship to the first man she had met in this wood but there was a marked and very reassuring difference in his attitude. There was neither resentment nor hostility in his easy acceptance of her presence.

Her eyes sparkled at him with rueful amusement. 'I seem to have lost myself,' she agreed lightly, responding readily to the singularly sweet smile that touched his grey eyes to such pleasing warmth.

Leisurely, Giles strolled to the edge of the lake to join the unknown girl and the dog who was nuzzling her as though she was a long-lost friend.

'These woods can be deceptive,' he said in his light, quiet way. 'It's very easy to lose one's way. Did you come in from Melling?'

Elfrida hesitated. 'Actually, I've walked from Frisby.'

'Then you are well out of your way.' He cuffed the dog affectionately.

'Down, Nero! I must apologize for his manners! He's just an overgrown pup and I'm having the devil's own job to train him. Down, boy!'

'I think he's mistaken me for someone else,' Elfrida said, smiling. 'No, we aren't old friends, you silly soft thing!' she addressed the dog with indulgent amusement, rubbing the silken ears.

'Obviously a case of love at first sight,' Giles commented, his eyes alive with laughter.

Elfrida's own eyes danced as she looked up at him. 'He's gorgeous — but not very efficient as a guard dog! I'm sure that he's supposed to warn me off. After all, I *am* trespassing.' Her tone volunteered an apology.

'Oh, that doesn't matter. Everyone is welcome to enjoy the woods for my part,' Giles said carelessly. 'I'm Giles Inskip, by the way.' He smiled down at her with a hint of enquiry in his grey eyes.

'Hendry . . . Elfrida Hendry,' she said

and impulsively held out her hand, liking him, hoping to know more of him. She was pleased that his clasp, warm and firm, gave no hint of lingering although she knew from the warmth of admiration in his eyes that he also hoped that friendship would spring from a chance meeting.

'Hendry,' he repeated. 'The name seems to be familiar. But we haven't met before, I know. I wouldn't have forgotten you,' he said simply.

A little flush of pleasure stole into her face at the implied compliment. 'No, we haven't met,' she agreed. 'Perhaps you've heard of my father — Owen Hendry. He writes. We've rented a cottage in Frisby for a few months.'

'Then you're new to the district? Oh, it's a very pretty part of England. You must let me show it off to you,' he suggested, not too eagerly but with just the right degree of easy friendliness. 'Nero! Down!' he commanded, abruptly realizing Elfrida's efforts to avoid having her face washed by a heavy pink tongue. He spoke so vehemently that the dog was startled into instant obedience. 'His manners are appalling . . . I'm so sorry,' Giles apologized with his sweet smile. 'I hope he didn't tear your dress,' he added in swift concern.

Elfrida surveyed the rent in her skirt without anxiety. 'I caught it on a bramble. It's quite ancient so it doesn't matter.' She smiled at him. 'I'm so glad you came along. I seem to have been walking in circles for ages. I expect I should have sunk to the ground in utter exhaustion eventually!'

'Not to be found till many years from now when my grandchildren rushed into tea with a most unlikely story of a skeleton in the undergrowth,' he agreed, his eyes twinkling.

She laughed. 'Gruesome thought! Anyway, I'm obviously not as far from civilization as I supposed. So if you could just point me in the right direction . . . ?'

'I've a much better idea,' he said

firmly. 'It's only a short walk to the house and I'm sure you would like some tea and afterwards I'll run you to the village in my car. I expect you've had enough walking for one day.'

'Thank you — but I really must get back as soon as possible,' Elfrida said with equal firmness, her tone reminding him that they were still strangers. 'My father will be getting anxious about me.'

It was a pity to dash the eagerness from his good-looking face and she doubted if her father, engrossed in his work, would have yet recalled her existence but she instinctively rejected Giles Inskip's suggestion. It was very likely that she would meet his brothers and there was one in particular that she did not wish to meet again — at least, not until she once more resembled the elegant, self-possessed and much-admired Elfrida Hendry and could not again be mistaken for a gipsy, she thought with resentment still burning in her breast.

'Then I'd better show you the way to Naylors Farm which you must have passed. If we cut across their meadow it will bring us to the outskirts of the village. Heel, Nero!'

He obviously meant to escort her for part of the way and Elfrida decided that she would be glad of his company. As they walked, talking lightly on a variety of subjects, she warmed even more to him and she raised no objection to his easy assumption that they would spend the golden days of summer in each other's company for much of the time. He happily outlined a variety of plans for her entertainment in the coming weeks and Elfrida was thankful to have found a friend. He was goodlooking and personable and quite eligible enough to satisfy her over-protective father — and she was woman enough to be flattered by his unmistakable admiration.

They reached the road that linked the village of Frisby with the town of Melling and began the last stretch of their walk. Nero bounded ahead until he was called to heel at the sound of an approaching car which passed them, a moment later, rather too fast for the narrow road, raising a cloud of dust and almost forcing them into the ditch.

Giles glowered in the wake of the car and then turned to Elfrida with an apology in his eyes. 'That maniac was one of my brothers, I'm sorry to say!'

Elfrida had not seen the driver but she knew instinctively that it was the brother she had already met. Her dislike of him abruptly hardened. She thought that driving dangerously on a narrow country road was exactly what she would expect from a man so arrogant, so aggressive.

'He doesn't seem to give a damn for anyone who gets in his way,' she said with a slight edge to her tone.

'There are days when the devil is in him,' Giles said wryly. But he added with swift regret for the moment of disloyalty: 'Yet when he chooses there's no one with more charm than Luke!'

Elfrida's mouth tightened fractionally. There was no need to mention her brief encounter with Luke Inskip but she was very sure that he would not redeem himself in her eyes no matter how charming he might be — when he chose!

2

The unpredictable Owen Hendry was leaning on the low gate, smoking his pipe and enjoying a comfortable gossip with an elderly neighbour, when Elfrida and Giles reached the cottage.

All unwittingly, he bore out Elfrida's claim by declaring loudly: 'There you are, child! I was getting anxious about you . . . beginning to think you might be lost!'

She exchanged smiles with Giles. 'But I have been lost,' she said lightly. 'Fortunately I was found and brought safely home.'

Owen's shrewd eyes rested on the young man and assessed him swiftly. He liked what he saw. 'You're an Inskip,' he said abruptly. 'No mistaking that colouring or those looks. Knew your father years ago. Know one of your brothers, too . . . can't recall his name.

Moody fellow.' He shot out a hand. 'I'm Owen Hendry. Daresay your father may have mentioned my name.'

'Yes, indeed, sir,' Giles said promptly. 'I'm pretty sure that he stocked the library with your books, too. He was proud to claim acquaintance with you.' There was a glimmer of amusement as well as reproach in the sparkling glance that Elfrida sent him but he met her eyes with bland innocence. 'I can't claim to know your work, sir,' he went on with disarming candour. 'I'm not much of a reader. But I have seen you on television, of course.'

'You've been taking care of my girl, have you? Much obliged to you! I'm glad she's finding some friends . . . we're new to the district as I expect she has told you. Come in and have some tea with us!'

Giles hesitated, glancing at Elfrida. She seconded the invitation with a smile and he said swiftly: 'Thank you, sir — I will!'

'Bring the dog. I don't mind dogs,'

Owen said in his abrupt but kindly way. He led the way into the cottage, plying the young man with eager questions.

At the first opportunity, Elfrida slipped away to her room to take stock of her appearance and make some rapid improvement. She told herself wryly that she looked as though she had been through a hedge backwards and annoyed beyond all reason, she swiftly set about transforming a careless girl into an elegant young woman.

She was rewarded for her efforts by the swift catch of Giles Inskip's breath when she joined him in the small sitting-room some minutes later. She wore a simple but well-cut dress of cream linen and the orange scarf about her throat exactly matched the lipstick which was a perfect foil for the sun-kissed skin and the tawny, gold-flecked eyes. Her thick curls were drawn into a smooth, sleek knot on the nape of her slender neck.

Giles had thought her a very pretty girl. He was taken aback by the discovery that she was a beautiful woman. She must have a dozen admirers hoping for her attention and it had been stupid of him to suppose that she would want to spend her days in his company, he thought ruefully, getting instinctively to his feet at her entry and feeling suddenly unsure of himself.

Nero lifted his head from his paws, thumping his tail in friendly greeting. Elfrida bent down to pull the dog's ears before she sat down on the sofa, smiling at Giles. 'Oh, don't stand on ceremony,' she said lightly but she was pleased with the effect she had achieved. She turned her attention to the tea tray that stood on a low table. 'I didn't know you were on your own. What happened to Owen?'

'He said something about cake and dashed out of the room,' Giles said, a little diffidently.

'He's been sidetracked,' Elfrida said shrewdly. 'Suddenly thought of a telling phrase and hurried to write it down, I expect. He won't think about the cake again. I don't think we have any, anyway.'

'It doesn't matter,' Giles assured her, amused and feeling rather more relaxed. He took the cup she offered and said with faint curiosity: 'Forgive me but do you always call your father by his first name?'

'Oh, always,' she said blithely. 'He prefers it.' She twinkled at him. 'Does it shock you? We aren't very conventional people.'

'Disregard for the conventions must be infectious,' he said, a little wryly. 'When I was airily making plans for taking you here, there and everywhere, I quite overlooked the fact that we hardly know each other. I'm sure you must have a great many other claims on your time.'

'Oh dear! Have you changed your mind?' Elfrida asked lightly. 'I was relying on you to take me here, there and everywhere, too!' She smiled at him with impulsive warmth and added gently: 'Don't be put off by the glamour. It's only for effect!'

He laughed. 'And what effect! I'm knocked out! You're beautiful!'

'Yes,' she said simply. 'But that doesn't stop us from being friends, surely.'

Not quite knowing what to make of her, Giles said lightly: 'I shall be the envy of every man for miles around.' And particularly my brothers, he thought, wondering how long he could keep this enchanting girl to himself.

She shook her head, smiling . . . and he was pleased to discover that though she might well be aware of her beauty she did not place undue importance on its impact. His liking for her had grown while they walked to the village, finding that they had much in common. Now he realized that a chance encounter with a stranger had given him a great deal to think about.

Giles was not a womanizer like his brothers. There had been one or two girls in his affections but no serious affairs. He was a modest young man for all his good looks and he was embarrassed when women expected him to enjoy flirtation just because he was an Inskip. It was a relief to meet a girl who seemed to accept him as a friend and would not expect him to play the lover. They could be friends and companions and enjoy some good times together without making demands on each other's emotions, Giles felt. Perhaps love would grow out of a deepening affection for each other as the weeks passed. But Giles felt that loving was synonymous with dedicating the rest of his life to a woman and it was such a serious decision to make that he did not mean to rush headlong into love with any girl — and he was confident from the little he already knew of Elfrida Hendry that she was not the type to indulge in romantic dreams of love at first sight.

It was an accurate assessment. Elfrida was impulsive with her affections but she did not believe in love at first sight. She was not too sure that she believed in love at all, having observed its disastrous effects on the heads and hearts of several of her friends. She supposed that the day might dawn when one man in particular seemed dearer to her than any other and made her long to spend the rest of her life with him. But she knew she had not met him yet and it might be many years before she did. In the meantime, she liked male company and male attention but always played fair. She did not encourage any man to fall in love with her and she did not deliberately fan the flames of any man's ardour. That was playing with fire, in her view. She liked to be kissed and she could respond with enjoyment to a man's embrace but she brought a light touch to her affairs and managed to refuse the more ardent of her admirers without offending them. The kind of relationship that Giles Inskip appeared to be offering would suit her very well, she felt, sensing that he regarded love between a man and a woman in much the same light that she did ... something to be approached with care and caution and entered into only after a great deal of consideration and with marriage in mind.

So she smiled on him with warmth and very real liking and looked forward to the pleasure of his company with the firm conviction that their friendship would not lead to any unwelcome or foolish complications ... and they parted with the agreement that they would spend most of the following day in exploring the countryside beyond Inskip.

Giles walked home in a thoughtful and quietly happy frame of mind. Even Nero failed to incur more than an absent reporach when he paused to continue a longstanding argument with the Naylor dogs.

He reached the Manor just as Luke came striding around the corner of the rambling old house. The two brothers met by the main door and Giles took the opportunity to reproach Luke for his lack of care on the roads. 'You damn nearly put me in the ditch and you might have killed Nero!' he said with more heat than was usual with him.

Luke raised an amused eyebrow. 'Oh, was that you, little brother?' he drawled. 'I thought you had more sense than to stroll in the middle of the road as though cars hadn't yet been invented!'

Giles flushed slightly. 'That doesn't alter the fact that you were driving much too fast,' he accused. 'Where the devil were you going in such a hurry, anyway?'

'To fetch John Barry to Miranda. She dropped her foal this afternoon and I couldn't get through on the phone . . . a fault on the line or something. We needed him urgently.' He strode through the hall to the library and Giles hurried after him.

'Miranda! Is she all right?' he demanded swiftly, anxiously, his grievance forgotten.

'She'll do. The foal died.' Luke spoke curtly, indifferently.

But Giles knew that it had hit him

very hard to lose the foal on which so many hopes had been built. His horses meant a great deal to Luke Inskip. 'Lord, I'm sorry,' he said warmly. 'But what went wrong? Miranda was fine when I looked her over this morning.'

Luke poured whisky from a decanter into a glass and swirled the liquid for a moment or two, staring into its amber depths, before he tossed it off abruptly. He glanced at his brother and his expression was very grim. 'Someone took her out this afternoon. I found her loose in a field in a very distressed condition. She'd been ridden hard by someone who either didn't know or care that she was due to foal very shortly.'

'My God!' Giles said slowly, his eyes dark with horror. 'But who would do such a thing?'

'Gipsies camped last night in Lower Mill Meadow,' Luke said harshly, refilling his glass. 'The devil of it is that I've no proof. I can only hit out at the bloody inefficient people who were supposed to be responsible for the mare. But I'll have those vermin off my land by nightfall if I have to take a rifle to them!'

Gilies was silent, a little alarmed. Luke was quite capable of carrying out his threat and he had very good reason to hold the gipsy people in aversion. For his part, Giles quite liked the travellers but he did not dare to speak of them beneath the roof of his home.

'I came across one of them in the woods,' Luke went on, throwing himself into a chair. 'I thought I'd scared the hell out of them the last time they were in the district.' He drained his glass and set it down on a low table close to his hand. Then he threw back his head and closed his eyes and Giles quietly withdrew from the room, knowing that his brother desperately needed a few minutes of solitude.

Giles was ten years younger than Luke and very different in type and temperament. He was a thoughtful and caring young man who was very much liked for his quiet courtesy, his cheerful good humour, his genuine interest in and concern for other people. Luke hadn't a care for anybody, wild and reckless, going his own way with arrogant disregard for everything but his own wishes, his own desires, his own feelings.

Giles had all the makings of an excellent squire but he had not succeeded to that rôle — or its problems, he often thought with thankfulness. He did not envy Luke the difficult and demanding job of managing the estate affairs and juggling with finances. He played his part with his brothers in running the estate, being responsible for the maintenance and repairs of the farms and outbuildings and cottages that they owned. It was a job that he enjoyed. He liked to be out and about, meeting people, listening to problems and putting things right where he could, and he could not have borne the long hours of desk work that fell to Luke's lot more often than not.

Luke carried a great deal of responsibility and he worked very hard. Perhaps it was scarcely surprising that he was a wild devil when he set aside the cares of the estate for a few hours. But he was a moody fellow. Very charming when he chose and bloody-minded for much of the time. Men seldom liked him but never failed to respect him — and women liked him much too much. Or so Giles thought, deploring the scandals in which his brother was too often involved. Arrogant devil, the women declared — and preened their feathers if he so much as glanced in their direction! His affairs were numerous and usually brief. For Luke was not a marrying man and made it plain.

Giles left the house and made his way to the stables where he spent some time talking to the groom who was responsible for Miranda and had undoubtedly felt the rough edge of his brother's tongue that afternoon. He learned that the man was under notice and was not surprised for Luke had a quick temper but he could not believe that his brother really meant to let Barney go. He had been with them for years and was very skilled and experienced and entirely to be trusted. Raging toothache had taken him to Melling for urgent dental attention and in his absence the stable lads had been too busy playing cards to notice that Miranda was missing from her stall. They had not seen or heard any strangers around the stables and everyone had been stunned when Luke strode through the archway with Miranda wearily hobbling beside him, lamed, distressed and about to give birth.

Barney was extremely upset and Giles stayed longer than he had intended but he left the man in a more hopeful frame of mind, having promised to talk to his brother. He called to Nero who was hobnobbing with the stable dogs and returned to the house to shower and dress for dinner.

It was a difficult meal. Luke was grim and virtually silent. Guy and Simon were sobered by the news that had greeted them on their return, one from Melling where he had been attending the weekly sale of stock and the other from the Home Farm where there had been a terrifying suspicion of foot and mouth disease that had thankfully been proved to be unfounded.

The twins were tall, good-looking, stamped with the Inskip colouring and the Inskip taste for the good things in life. But they did not have Luke's wildness to such an extent any more than they were as thoughtful and responsible as Giles. They worked hard and they played hard and neither of them were ready to settle down . . . but there was not an ounce of real vice in either of them.

Giles kept some degree of conversation flowing but never once mentioned the girl who was still very much on his mind. A suitable moment to introduce the subject of the Hendrys did not seem to arise.

Indeed, Giles was a little wary of

introducing Elfrida to his brothers at all. It was unavoidable, of course. But she was much too lovely and really very young. He could not help feeling slightly possessive and a little protective where she was concerned although they had so recently met that it seemed presumptuous. It would be childish to claim that he had met her first but he suspected that he would need to be constantly reminding his brothers of the fact once they had met Elfrida Hendry. Guy and Simon were light-hearted flirts and he did not doubt that she was experienced enough in rebuffing that kind of attention. There was little to fear from the twins. But Luke was the real threat, Giles thought wryly. He was undeniably very attractive to women and his careless treatment that almost bordered on indifference only appeared to make him all the more desirable in a woman's eyes. Giles could only hope that his brother would not take one of his rare fancies to Elfrida — or that she would be one of the few women who did not fall under his spell at sight.

There was little doubt that Luke was a dangerous man for a young girl to know, Giles felt, innate chivalry stirring. But he comforted himself with the thought that Elfrida was not likely to appeal to a man like Luke. She was beautiful and that might briefly attract his notice. But she was not the type of girl to welcome his brand of loving and Luke had no time to waste on innocents . . .

3

Elfrida was restless and a little bored. Perhaps it was reaction after the pleasurable excitement of meeting and getting to know a rather attractive man but the evening hours seemed to stretch ahead with little to fill them.

Impulsively encouraging her father to rent this cottage in the enchanting village that they had both liked on sight, she had quite overlooked the fact that she would be many miles from the metropolis that she knew and loved and that she would have no friends in the district and it would take time to make some. She had optimistically supposed that the village and the country town of Melling and the coastal resort only twelve miles away would supply all her needs for the summer. But she had forgotten that she was not by nature a solitary person and it had not occurred to her that a village was a close community that did not welcome strangers very readily. Her father had managed to chip away a little of the natural reserve that seemed to typify their new neighbours and the vicar had called as well as a rather formidable lady who demanded of her father if he played bridge and seemed to lose interest as soon as she discovered that he did not.

They were neither fish nor fowl nor good red herring, Elfrida had told herself ruefully. The villagers were prepared to be pleasant but obviously considered the writer and his daughter socially above them. And until her meeting with Giles that day, it had seemed that the Inskips meant to ignore the advent of the Hendrys.

She felt rather more hopeful now that she knew Giles. Her friendship with him must surely open other doors in the district and perhaps she would not need to mourn her lack of friends in the very near future. But that did not

provide her with any source of entertainment on this particular evening, she
thought, wandering from room to
room, indoors and outdoors and back
again, distracting her father who had
settled down with his beloved books
and was much too self-sufficient, too
insular, to care for the social life that his
daughter thought so necessary to her
well-being.

She sighed for the tenth time and
tossed aside the magazine that she had
riffled through with very little interest.
She poured herself another cup of
coffee and discovered it to be cold. She
toyed with the idea of telephoning some
of her town friends and then decided
that they would not be at home at this
hour of the evening.

She wandered into the garden and
tugged half-heartedly at a weed or two.
She talked to the neighbour's cat who
stalked off without deigning to reply.
She looked up and down the quiet
village street and then across at the
village pub, just a few yards distant.

Several cars were parked in the forecourt and she supposed that it was all happening at the Dog and Duck if nowhere else. But she lacked the courage to run the gamut of all those strangers who would certainly stare if she entered on her own.

Abruptly her eyes brightened. For a tall man came out of the pub, his auburn hair gleaming bright in the evening sunshine. Elfrida's heart lifted with the hope that it was Giles and she waited for him to turn his face in her direction.

He was followed immediately by a swarthy man who was several inches shorter and all the more pugnacious because of his lack of height. Glaring, he voiced a stream of filthy abuse ... and the man he addressed spun swiftly on his heel, his fists clenching.

The swift confrontation with all its obvious intent informed Elfrida that she had mistaken the man's identity. For Giles was the last man to be involved in a public brawl, she was sure.

41

Whereas it was exactly what she would expect of his impossible brother!

The swarthy little man struck out wildly, more drunk than sober, and was instantly felled by a short, sharp blow from the other man's fist. But he was back on his feet in a moment with a trickle of blood at the corner of his mouth and wildness in his eyes and fresh obscenities on his lips. Luke knew how to handle himself on these occasions but he was not prepared for a foul blow that bent him double. A chop on the back of his neck brought him to his knees and a couple of hefty kicks from a well-aimed boot sent him sprawling — and before he could recover his breath or his senses, his attacker was behind the wheel of his broken-down lorry and away.

Elfrida was appalled. She had not wanted to witness the violence but it had all happened so swiftly that she had been mesmerized.

The street was deserted. One or two curious heads had appeared at the door of the pub but no one had chosen to interfere or to go to the assistance of the man on the ground. Without even thinking twice, Elfrida opened the gate and rushed across the road to his side, casting aside all consideration but compassion. She bent over him anxiously.

Luke was almost beside himself with pain and fury. Both his pride and his dignity had been trampled in the dirt of the pub courtyard — and he was damned if he needed a woman's help! He did not even look at her as he thrust her away and struggled to his feet. He leaned against the pub wall, glad of its support, bruised and sick and aware of an ugly pain in his ribs each time he breathed . . . and he glowered at the publican who finally ventured out to offer assistance.

'I didn't know what was going on till one of the lads called me,' he said apologetically. 'Come back in and I'll get you some brandy, Mr Luke. You're shaken up and no wonder. It's a matter for the police, too,' he added, rather reluctantly. He glanced at Elfrida, recognizing her. 'It's all right, miss . . . I'll see to the gentleman,' he said discouragingly.

'I'll settle my own score a damn sight quicker than the police will,' Luke said curtly. 'And it will be a long time before I set foot inside your doors again! You encourage every rogue and vagabond in the country to haunt the place, it seems to me!'

'Now, now, Mr Inskip,' the publican said, long-felt dislike beginning to show through. 'You shouldn't begin to blame me for what happened. The man was civil enough and sober enough and it seems to me that you deliberately provoked him to turn nasty!'

'I'll provoke him with a riding-crop the next time we meet,' Luke said savagely. He moved away from the supporting wall, staggered slightly, recovered and brushed past the still-hovering, still-concerned Elfrida as he made his way to his car. The publican looked after him for a moment, then shrugged and turned away, his expression seeming to indicate that he believed it high time *that* particular Inskip had his come-uppance . . .

Shocked by the man's indifference, Elfrida watched Luke Inskip walk rather unsteadily across the forecourt, thinking that he looked ill and in pain. She had been annoyed by his brusque rejection of her desire to help but she could recognize a man in an ungovernable rage when she saw one and she was ready to make allowances.

Luke paused for a moment by the car, an arm nursing his throbbing rib-cage, and he shook his head slightly in an attempt to clear it before he ventured to drive back to the Manor.

Elfrida went over to him, prepared to meet with a rebuff but quite unable to ignore his obvious need of assistance. After all, he was Giles' brother and that fact alone must compel her concern. 'Are you sure that you're all right?' she asked, a little anxiously. 'Is there anything I can do for you?'

Luke looked at her, really seeing her for the first time, ready to thank her, however ungraciously. After all, it was a rare woman who got herself involved in such a situation. Then he recognized her and his eyes narrowed and his lip curled with instant contempt.

'I'll survive,' he said roughly. 'There's nothing you can do for me, darling — and thanks to your friend I'm in no shape to do anything for you,' he added with savage mockery, shaking her hand abruptly from his arm.

Words and tone left Elfrida in absolutely no doubt of the interpretation he had set on her good intentions. Her face flamed. Then, quite involuntarily, she slapped his face and saw mingled surprise and loathing leap to his grey eyes. She turned on her heel and stalked away from him, affront in every line of her slender body.

Luke looked after her briefly, startled by her response to his taunt, struck by something about her that gave him pause. But his churning anger and the pain of cracked ribs and the heavy throbbing of his head demanded more of his attention and he dismissed the girl from his mind as he gingerly eased himself behind the wheel and set the car in motion . . .

Elfrida slammed the cottage door in order to give vent to her feelings. She had never felt so angry, so outraged, in all her life! He was an impossible, detestable pig of a man! How dared he speak to her and look at her so! How dared he think ill of her in the first place! He was despicable! She had never disliked anyone so much in all her life! She never wanted to set eyes on him again!

It had been stupid to go to his aid. His brawls were none of her business, after all, and her liking for Giles did not oblige her to become involved in any way whatever with his unpleasant brother. No one else had gone to help Luke Inskip and she was not at all surprised, having discovered for herself that he was not a man who inspired liking or sympathy. It seemed to her that he had a wicked temper and would lash out at any one when it flared and it would be wise for everyone to give him a wide berth, especially when he had been drinking! It was very likely that he thoroughly deserved the beating he had just received, she told hereslf. The pub landlord had certainly not taken his side, reproaching him for provocation, in fact. That spoke for itself, Elfrida decided ... and determined that she would not think of him again ...

The gipsy caravans were gone with the dawn, obviously expecting trouble after the incident with the mare and the fight in the village. Luke surveyed the littered corner of the meadow where the caravans had stood, cold anger in his grey eyes.

There had been murder in his heart on the previous night but his brothers had persuaded him to leave matters till the morning. Now it was too late. The man he sought — and the girl — were gone.

Inexplicably he knew a slight heaviness of guilt about the girl. He had been brusque with her when he found her wandering in the woods but she had probably been doing no harm. Later, he had thrust her away with ill grace when she tried to help him, instinctively suspicious of all her tribe. Now, he fancied that she had been really concerned for him. He recalled the words that had provoked her to anger. She had slapped his face . . . the swift reaction of an indignant woman who resented the slur on her character and her morals. Perhaps he had misjudged her. But he had been too angry to think straight. He hated her kind and he refused to believe that there could be good in any of them.

And yet . . . There had been something about the girl which haunted him throughout a virtually sleepless night. Restless, bothered by the discomfort of strapped ribs, still angry over the loss of

49

Miranda's foal, filled with loathing for the nomadic people who had dared to venture on to Inskip land, he had tossed and turned — and found his mind constantly conjuring an image of the girl. It was her eyes that particularly haunted him, he discovered. Unusual eyes. Striking eyes in a small face that he recalled as rather lovely in the early hours of the morning.

She had been surprisingly clean and tidy for a gipsy girl. She had been surprisingly well spoken and he fancied that she had been surprisingly well dressed although his recollection was vague about her clothes. But she was every inch a gipsy with the black curls and brown skin and that proud defiance with all its latent hostility. She needed taming, he had decided grimly, recalling the hauteur with which she had struck him and then flounced away from him. Thinking of her with belated interest, his blood stirred for he was a sensual man and she had been unmistakably attractive. Deliberately, he dwelt with enjoyment on the prospect of taming her even though he had not the slightest real desire to meet her again. It was mere fantasizing to take his mind off the discomfort that was the direct result of her tribe's advent . . .

Now, he stared at the flattened and scorched grass and refused to admit that it had been desire for the girl rather than a wish to confront his attacker that had brought him so early to the meadow. He turned away, slashing savagely at the long grass with his crop.

'Wasting our time here,' he said roughly.

Giles nodded. 'They won't be back — not unless one of them is prepared to face a summons for assault!' He understood Luke's desire for a personal revenge but he felt that recourse to the law would be wiser.

'Damn them all!' Luke declared with sudden passion . . . and some of his anger was directed at himself for the disloyalty of his blood in wanting a gipsy girl. His voice shook with the force of his hatred for all her kind . . .

Giles was silent, sympathizing and yet knowing that Luke did not wish for any reference to the past. Luke never referred to that day, eight years before, when he had lost the woman he loved, soon to be his bride, because the gipsies had come to Frisby. It had been a tragedy for which no one had really been to blame yet Luke had blamed the gipsies and would not allow them within sight or sound of the Manor ever afterwards.

Sybil had been young and full of life, a madcap, wild and headstrong as Luke himself and dear to them all since childhood. But it was Luke she had loved and Luke she had meant to marry and all the arrangements were in hand for the wedding when the gipsies paused for a night or two in Frisby. For many years they had been tolerated if not exactly welcomed and Luke had taken little notice of the announcement that they were camped, as usual, in Lower Mill Meadow.

But Sybil had taken it into her lovely head to have her fortune told and, laughing and shaking her head to Luke's half-hearted protests, she had turned her mare in the direction of the gipsy encampment. With Luke in her wake, she had galloped full pelt across the field . . . and looked back to laugh a challenge, superb in the saddle. Too late, she had seen the child in her path . . . a toddler who emerged from a slight hollow clutching a wriggling puppy in her arms.

By some miracle, Sybil had avoided the child. But the panic-stricken dog, held in too tight a grasp, had finally struggled free and leaped to the ground in front of the mare, yelping. The highly-strung thoroughbred had reared, throwing its rider heavily to the ground.

Sybil had lain in coma for three days and Luke had scarcely left her side. When she died, he was a changed man . . . bitter, morose, bent on going to hell his own way.

He had been very young and deeply

in love and eagerly looking forward to his wedding day. Sybil had been his love. The many women in his life in the past eight years had been mere light of loves. He had not been seeking another woman to take Sybil's place in his heart, his life. He merely sought an ease for the longing and the loneliness and the need. He made no promises and did not believe that he broke any hearts. The most eligible bachelor in the district, he had no intention of marrying. He had learned to value his freedom and considered himself too self-sufficient to need any woman to the extent of wanting to share the rest of his life with her. In his view, women made too many demands if a man was fool enough to fall into the trap of loving. He would have been the happiest of men if he had married Sybil but she had been swept from his arms by a cruel destiny. There could never be another Sybil . . .

Memories and the memory of pain came flooding. He swung into the saddle of the black stallion and spurred him to movement, heading for open country without another word for his brother.

Giles looked after him in rueful understanding, knowing that someone would probably suffer because of the mood that was black as the horse . . .

4

Luke rode across the fields, his lean body one with the horse, his hair glinting in the bright sun . . . and the girl who sat on a five-barred gate, watching for him, saw him long before he was aware of her. Her heart quickened in eager anticipation and she waited, smiling, the soft colour of excitement in her pretty face.

As he drew nearer, she waved . . . and he raised a hand in acknowledgment of her. He drew rein as he neared the gate and Annabel jumped down from her perch and ran to meet him. 'Hi!' she called youthfully.

Luke dismounted and dropped the rein and caught the slender hands that she held out to him. 'Hallo, princess,' he said lightly, his mood lightening at the obvious warmth of affection in her greeting. He was very fond of Annabel.

In many ways, she reminded him of Sybil . . . and it was more than the family likeness between cousins.

'Surprised to see me?' she demanded, lifting her face for his kiss as she had done since she was a child.

'Home for the weekend?' he asked, brushing her lips so briefly with his own that she was disappointed.

'Home for good,' she amended. 'It didn't work out. Sharing a flat with three girls isn't me, I'm afraid.' She had been away for several weeks, living and working in London. But she had been homesick and not one of the many men she had met could compare satisfactorily with Luke.

'I didn't think it would be,' he reminded her, smiling.

'I missed all the spoiling I get here,' she said, dimpling, meaning that she had missed him.

'You're too pretty not to have had more than your fair share of spoiling . . . or are the men in London all blind?'

'I guess I just prefer the men in this part of the world,' Annabel returned lightly. And her coquettish glance implied that she referred to one man in particular.

He was amused. She had been trying to flirt with him ever since she could walk, he thought with indulgent and affectionate amusement. He suspected that she had been lying in wait for him this morning, knowing that he was expected at Ripley Hall.

She ought to know that he was a dangerous man for a young girl to become entangled with . . . and of course she knew. But Luke was well aware that girls of her age were very susceptible to the attractions of a rake. As it happened, she was too young and much too innocent to be in any danger from him. Yet, child though she was, she had all the promise of a woman, he thought idly, his glance running over the rounded contours beneath the jersey, the tiny waist and provocative little bottom in the tight jeans. He was in a reckless, devil-may-care mood . . . and he was bored with the woman of the moment. He would soon become bored with youthful naivete, too. But it might be amusing to gratify Annabel with a little attention. Nothing more. They were near neighbours and he did not believe in conducting his amorous affairs on his own doorstep. She was a nice child, a very pretty child, feminine and appealing . . . and he was drawn to her because she was a youthful edition of Sybil who was so much on his mind that morning.

'It's nice to have you back, anyway, infant,' he said carelessly.

'Missed me?' she asked swiftly, youthfully.

'I'm used to having you around,' he told her, smiling.

She studied him, trying to gauge the amount of sincerity behind the light words. 'I expect you didn't even notice that I was away,' she said sagely.

'You've been away so much,' he pointed out. 'School and college and finishing school . . . and every time you come home you seem to have grown up a little more. Now . . . ' He put a finger under her chin and tilted her face to smile into the trusting blue eyes. 'Now you're quite a woman,' he said softly.

Her heart missed a beat as she realized the meaningful glow in the grey eyes that could lighten or darken with his mood. She was thrilled but also just a little alarmed. He was very much a man of the world and, for all her much-vaunted experience, she was not sure that she could handle a man like Luke who had a reputation that people whispered about in corners. He was a rake, a womanizer. There had been some scandal concerning him and another man's wife . . . another concerning a girl he had reputedly refused to marry although she expected his child. Annabel was excited but apprehensive, knowing that it might be dangerous to encourage him. But he was very attractive and her foolish heart had yearned after him for ages . . .

'Oh, I'm quite grown up now,' she said impulsively, smiling at him with warm encouragement and just a hint of provocation in her blue eyes.

'It's been a long wait — but worth it,' he said with meaning and kissed her. Not as he had kissed her a few moments before but with a lingering and deliberate intent. He kissed her as he might kiss a woman who attracted him and Annabel's heart leaped into her throat and threatened to stay there. For the nineteen year old girl, not quite as sophisticated as she believed herself to be, had never been kissed in just that way by any of the young men who had been her flirts since she slipped into her teens.

Her thoughts raced with as much eager delight as her heart. For his words implied that she had a special place in his affections . . . that he had been waiting for her to grow up, in fact! Everyone said he was not a marrying man and that he was still in love with her dead cousin. But Annabel was young and romantic enough to dream of being the one woman who might take Sybil's place in his heart and in his life. It was eight years since Sybil had died and eight years was a very long time! Then she had been a child, Annabel thought soberly. Now she was a woman — and it seemed that Luke was suddenly aware of her just as she had always hoped . . .

'Wow!' she exclaimed youthfully as he released her and her eyes danced with delight.

'Wow indeed!' Luke said, laughing, a little relieved to discover that she had reacted with lightness to his kiss. Rather late, he thought it had been a mistake to kiss her at all . . .

'Have you come to breakfast?' she asked, tucking her hand into his arm as he caught Nimrod's rein and they turned to stroll towards the house.

'I came to see you,' he said promptly.

Her eyes twinkled. 'Liar! You didn't know I was home,' she teased.

'Of course I did. Giles is a very

reliable source of information.' And more suited to this little baggage by virtue of age and temperament, he thought soberly.

Annabel regarded him thoughtfully. 'So you did miss me?'

'Desperately,' he said mendaciously, his eyes twinkling.

'That explains all the phone calls and letters and constant trips to town to see me,' she said demurely.

'I didn't think you'd have time for me,' he returned smoothly. 'And I refuse to stand in line with a dozen others. If you want me you'll have to disappoint all your other admirers, Annabel.'

'You're an incorrigible flirt,' she told him severely but her heart had bumped with sudden hope at the light words. 'How does a woman ever know when you're serious!'

'I'm never serious,' he said lightly. 'Be warned, princess.'

She pouted prettily. 'You treat me like a child!'

He touched her soft cheek in a little caress. 'I'm protecting you,' he said quietly. 'There's no harm in flirtation. It's just a game we can both enjoy. But don't get emotionally involved, Annabel. I'm not the man for you. I'm too old for you — and that's only one of the reasons why I won't encourage you to want me.'

'Perhaps you don't really want *me*,' she murmured provocatively, the warmth of womanhood in her very blue eyes as she looked up at him.

Luke could never resist that kind of challenge. And he was much too sensual not to be stirred by her prettiness, her femininity. He was also very conscious of her likeness to Sybil and this was one of those days when memories and the memory of pain came flooding.

'I ought not to want you,' he said wryly. But he drew her towards him and sought her lips with a sudden hunger that made him too reckless to remember her youth and her innocence . . .

Later that morning, Luke rode towards home, wondering if the mood of the moment had led him into something he would swiftly regret. He was not proud of the impulse that had urged him to make love to a nineteen year old innocent who trusted him and was a little too eager to fancy herself in love with him. She was very sweet, very appealing . . . and much too young. It would be wise to end a foolish flirtation as swiftly as it had begun. But he had committed himself to escorting her to the gala dance at the country club on Saturday and it would be impossible to disappoint her. Perhaps there was no harm in a light-hearted affair while it pleased her to think him more attractive than any of the attentive young men who would no doubt wish him on the other side of the world when they saw Annabel in his company!

He entered the big house, having left Nimrod with a groom, and halted abruptly as a girl he immediately recognized turned from the contemplation of his father's portrait that hung above the big fireplace in the hall.

Anger, black as night, darkened his grey eyes. 'What the hell are you doing here? What the devil do you want?'

Elfrida turned to look at him, her chin tilting. She had accompanied Giles into the house with reluctance, disliking the thought of meeting his unpleasant brother. Now she knew how justified she had been in not wishing to meet him again. 'I am here by invitation,' she said tautly.

'Not my invitation!' he snapped, scowling.

'Elfrida is my guest,' Giles said gently, running down the wide staircase with his jacket slung over his shoulder. Coming out of his room just as Luke entered the house, he had been startled and dismayed by the interchange between two people he supposed to be strangers to each other. Now he halted on the bottom stair and looked from his brother to Elfrida and back again, puzzled by their obvious antagonism. Luke's mood was very black and a nerve jumped in his lean cheek as he glowered at the girl who faced him with anger and a hint of outrage in her own eyes.

'Get her out of this house!' Luke said ominously, addressing his brother in curt command.

Giles stiffened. 'You forget your manners, old fellow,' he said lightly but the rebuke was unmistakable. 'I take it you know each other and presumably you have some quarrel that I know nothing about. But Elfrida is a friend of mine and I've invited her to lunch . . . '

'She doesn't eat beneath my roof!' Luke declared savagely.

'You're out of your mind . . . ' Giles began, his even temper threatening to desert him.

Elfrida touched his arm. 'Leave it,' she said quietly, very angry, high colour in her cheeks. 'It doesn't matter, Giles.'

'By God, it does matter!' Giles was suddenly as furious as his brother. He strode towards him, his eyes glinting, his jaw jutting pugnaciously and his fists clenching involuntarily. 'Apologize to the lady — or I'll bloody well make you!'

Luke's lip curled. '*Lady* . . . ' he echoed sneeringly. 'I think not.' His tone as well as the raking glance was a deliberate insult. 'She isn't welcome here and I'm astonished that you should invite her to this house, knowing my views on all her kind.'

Elfrida's own temper suddenly soared. Stupid man! For some reason he was determined to think of her as a gipsy and he obviously felt great animosity towards them. It was all a silly misunderstanding. There was really no need for him to be so deliberately offensive, she decided angrily, her dislike of him growing by the moment.

Giles was stunned, too taken aback even to deliver the blow that his brother certainly deserved. He could only stare at Luke, suddenly gone mad.

Elfrida said lightly but with anger

below the surface: 'Giles, your impossible brother mistakes me for someone else.'

'No mistake,' Luke said roughly, striding to the heavy front door and throwng it open in obvious implication. 'I know you for what you are — and I want you *out*!'

'Oh, you fool!' Elfrida flared, unable to hold her temper a moment longer. 'Do I really look like a gipsy? How can you be so stupid!'

Giles stared from one to the other in utter astonishment.

Luke, taken aback by her vehemence, looked at her for the first time . . . and realized the justice of her words. She did not look at all like a gipsy girl except in her vivid and very attractive colouring. In the very elegant cream suit and matching silk shirt, her hair worn in a knot on the nape of her neck, her loveliness enhanced by the very skilful application of make-up, she looked and obviously was a woman of breeding.

He had leaped to a false conclusion and insulted her into the bargain, he thought wryly. He could not help feeling just as much of a fool as she declared that he was . . . and he did not like the feeling. And he did not like her for inflicting it on him, however justified she might be. No woman had ever spoken to him in that particular way before. No woman had ever looked at him with such cold contempt or dismissed him so scornfully and it was an experience he did not enjoy or appreciate.

'Well?' Elfrida persisted indignantly. 'Do I?'

Giles found his voice at last. 'A gipsy! No! Luke, you surely didn't think I'd bring a gipsy girl here . . . to *this* house! You must be mad. Elfrida and her father have taken Clare Cottage for the summer . . . they are our new neighbours!'

Luke ignored him. He closed the heavy door and leaned with his back against it and regarded Elfrida with cold eyes. 'It seems I owe you an apology,' he said formally and with very little grace. 'I am sorry. There are reasons why I do not welcome gipsies on my land as my brother will no doubt explain. We met in circumstances that led me to think you were one of the tribe camping in one of my fields. Apparently I have been too hasty.'

Elfrida looked at him without trace of forgiveness or acceptance of the grudging apology. Then she turned to Giles. 'I think that lunch is out of the question, after all. Don't you? Perhaps you would take me home, Giles.' The smile she bestowed on him was in marked contrast to the cold contempt that was all his brother deserved.

'Yes, indeed!' Giles was mortified. He was furious with Luke and most upset that someone he had invited to the Manor, gipsy or not, should have met with such a reception from his brother. He would not forgive Luke in a hurry.

He could not understand how the mistake had happened . . . and he was puzzled and a little disappointed that Elfrida had not mentioned her previous encounter with Luke. 'I'll settle my score with you later, Luke,' he said grimly, putting a protective arm about Elfrida and ushering her towards the door.

A little smile flickered in Luke's eyes. It amused him to imagine the gentle, easy-going and sweet-natured Giles settling a score with anyone. 'Certainly,' he said lightly, moving away from the door.

Elfrida did not even glance at him as she left the house. Her head was high and there was a bright spark of indignation in her eyes and a firm resolve in her heart that she and Luke Inskip would never be on amicable terms, come what may!

Luke did not wait to see them drive away in Giles' small car. He turned away with a shrug that implied his complete indifference to the incident and the girl. It did not matter to him what she thought of him and, in retrospect, it was astonishing to recall that he had spent much of the night thinking about her . . .

5

Elfrida sat beside Giles in the small car as he drove her back to Frisby. She was struggling with a very natural desire to have nothing more to do with any of the Inskips.

Giles was very quiet and obviously troubled. She liked him too much to allow his beastly brother to spoil the easy and pleasant relationship which already promised so much for the future.

She reached to touch him lightly on the arm. He turned his head and she smiled at him with reassuring warmth. 'Don't be upset,' she said gently. 'It was just a silly misunderstanding. Forget it, Giles.'

'I don't know what to say to you,' he said unhappily. 'I can only apologize for my brother. He has this hatred of gipsies that makes him utterly

74

unreasonable if one ever crosses his path. Oh, not without reason,' he hastened to add. 'The girl he was going to marry died in a riding accident that was caused by gipsies camping in Lower Mill Meadow. He is a very unforgiving man and he is bitter and hostile towards all gipsies as a result . . . not surprisingly, perhaps. But I can't imagine why he took you for a gipsy.'

'Just leaping to conclusions,' she said lightly. 'He's very quick-tempered, isn't he?'

'I suppose so,' Giles conceded. 'We all are, I'm afraid . . . it's a family trait.'

She smiled at him, doubting that his temper, however swiftly ignited, could be as nasty as his brother's appeared to be. 'Do you get on well with him?' she asked curiously.

Smarting at the way Luke had spoken to him before a virtual stranger, Giles could still leap swiftly to his defence. 'We're the best of friends,' he said with instinctive loyalty. 'Don't be too hard on Luke . . . I told you he has good reason to dislike the gipsies. If he really thought you were one of them then it was impossible for him to pull his punches. But I'm sure he regrets the way he treated you.'

'I should have mentioned that I'd met him,' Elfrida said lightly. 'But it wasn't a very pleasant encounter and I wanted to forget it. And I couldn't be sure that it was your brother I'd seen in the woods although you are alike.'

She gave him a brief account of that original meeting and also sketched in the details of his fight with the gipsy outside the pub and her impulsive offer of assistance, so brusquely rejected. She made light of the incident, leaving out the final insult which would certainly incense the gentle Giles. She did not feel that there was anything to be gained by causing hostility between brothers.

'And I hoped you might be friends,' Giles said wryly. 'You have no reason to like Luke, however.' Deep down, he felt relief for he had feared that she might find Luke attractive, as did most women who came in his way.

'No reason at all,' Elfrida agreed, smiling. 'But I don't have to like him, do I? Only to please you, perhaps — and I'll try to like him if you want it. But don't ask me just yet!'

He laughed. 'No, I won't. I'll give you both time to cool down before I attempt to throw you together again!'

That was certainly the intention. But he did not know when he took Elfrida to the gala dance at the country club that his brother would be there with Annabel . . .

Giles felt a distinct thrill of pride as he entered the portals of the club with the beautiful Elfrida on his arm, knowing that heads turned and he was the envy of all his friends.

Elfrida was aware that she looked her best in the gown that graduated from palest lemon to deepest orange in layer after layer of whirling tulle, cut low to reveal the gentle swell of her breasts, baring the shapely shoulders and plunging deep in the back. Her black hair was piled high in a knot of curls, empress-fashion, threaded with ribbons of palest lemon to match the bodice of her gown. She was sparkling with delight in the evening, looking forward to meeting his friends, glad to be back in a social whirl again. And Giles was proud to be her escort and delighted to make her known to the people who crowded round in unmistakable admiration.

Luke stood at the bar, listening with only half an ear to Annabel's chatter. He was already a little bored and he wondered what had possessed him to begin a flirtation with naive youth. He was not so desperate that he needed to rob cradles!

Looking very pretty in the cornflower blue dress that complemented her eyes, Annabel talked and smiled, unaware of his disinterest, thoroughly enjoying herself. She preened in the confident conviction that every girl in the room was watching and wondering and envying her the attentions of the eligible and very attractive Luke Inskip.

His attention was drawn to the group of people near the door . . . and interest quickened as his glance fell on the girl in the striking gown. He was all man and he could not be indifferent to the picture she presented. She was superb, he decided, overshadowing every other woman with the dark beauty that caught the immediate attention. Giles was walking tall, Luke thought with indulgent amusement — and who could blame him? Such a woman would go to any man's head and she was playing up to Giles very prettily, allowing him and everyone else to assume that she had eyes for no other man in the room.

Luke could not help comparing the lovely creature in the flaming dress with the shabby urchin of the woods and marvelling that they were one and the same. She was a chameleon, he decided, intrigued and attracted.

As though she sensed his gaze, those incredible eyes were briefly turned towards him. Her glance swept over him and away as though he did not exist. A little smile flickered in his eyes. So she did not think him a force to reckon with. How little she knew of him! They had begun badly but there was a long way to go before the ending — and he was determined that indifference should give way to wanting . . .

'Who is that girl?' Annabel demanded, chagrined to realize that he had ceased to give her even a fraction of his attention. Like almost every man in the place, he was gazing at the newcomer as though he was bewitched, she thought crossly.

Reminded of her existence, Luke smiled down at her with careless warmth. 'My little brother's new girl-friend,' he said lightly. 'Very attractive, isn't she? I doubt if Giles will be able to hold on to her, though. Too many counter-claims in the offing,' he added drily, observing the men who flocked to demand an introduction to the lovely Elfrida. She would be overwhelmed with attentions. A new face was always of interest and this was a particularly beautiful face with a body to match.

Luke wanted her with sudden urgency and knew that he had been unable to put her completely out of his mind for days. She had been a tantalizing memory. He ought not to want a girl who belonged to his brother but rules were made to be broken and the intensity of his desire told him that his determination to have Elfrida overcame all brotherly considerations. But he did not mean to rush his fences . . .

Annabel half-expected that he would make a move to join the group about Giles and the girl. It would be entirely in character for him to whisk the beautiful newcomer from his brother and she did not doubt that he could succeed. He could be irresistible when he chose to exert his famous charm, she thought wryly. Glancing at him as he looked at the girl, she saw something in his eyes that caused a contraction of anxiety about her heart.

Sensing her gaze, Luke turned and smiled into her troubled blue eyes. 'Nose out of joint, princess?' he teased gently. 'You may lose some of your admirers but you're still the prettiest girl in the county for my money!'

The soft warmth that suffused her pretty face betrayed her pleasure at the compliment. He might not mean any of the sweet nothings but it was nice for a girl to hear them, she thought youthfully. And he had a gift for making a girl feel that she was the only woman in his world . . . however temporarily! His attractive smile and expressive eyes and lazy drawl were very convincing when one wanted so much to be convinced.

Of course he was skilled at flirtation and a man who pursued women for pleasure must be smoothly persuasive and possess a great deal of charm as well as physical attractiveness. He was undoubtedly a rake. But he had to settle down one day, she thought with all the optimism of her youth. If he could turn away from the kind of woman who had just entered on his brother's arm, seemingly indifferent, then perhaps he was tiring of the kind of sophisticated beauty who had always attracted him in the past. Perhaps there was real hope for herself, after all. For a man might lightly love a dozen beautiful women but eventually fall deeply in love with the girl next door — and she was certainly that!

Luke was very attentive and no one could have supposed that it was just a game to him as he danced with the pretty Annabel, his cheek against the soft hair with its teasing perfume. He was a sensual man and Annabel was a delight in his arms. He was too mature, too experienced, too worldly for such a young girl and it was not his intention to seduce her but there was pleasure to be gained from the moment and he was not a man to deny himself the gifts that the gods offered . . .

Giles was kept too busy fending off the so-called friends who sought to take Elfrida from him to realize his brother's presence. With laughing protest, she clung to his arm and refused to be parted from him, accepting compliments with smiling grace, agreeing to consider the invitations that were showered upon her, promising that she would dance with each and every one who asked in due course. But first she wanted a drink and then she wanted to dance with Giles and the evening was still young.

It was all great fun and Elfrida was enjoying herself as any woman would in such circumstances. But she seemed to have some kind of unwelcome sensitivity to the presence of Luke Inskip. She had known he was present even before her glance found him. A little dismayed, she was determined that he should not spoil her evening. But it was an awkward situation. He was Giles' brother and they would eventually be forced into tolerating each other. For the moment he was ignoring her and that was just the way she wanted it. Only once had she looked his way, flickering her eyes briefly over him and away so that he should not doubt her lack of interest.

Determined to forget her dislike of the man in the enjoyment of his brother's company, she nevertheless continued to be infuriatingly aware of him. It was odd that he should so dominate the big room, among all the people present. He had that kind of personality, she conceded. He had the looks, the build, the presence that could not fail to draw attention. It need not make him popular, merely impressive. And it obviously did impress the young girl who inflated his ego by hanging on his every word and gazing up at him in blatant adoration, Elfrida decided drily, a little surprised that his taste should run to such a foolish little creature. She would have supposed that a man of his age and undoubted experience would seek the company of a more mature woman. Surely such youthful adulation must bore him very swiftly! His kind of man liked a woman to be a challenge rather than a too-easy conquest, she suspected.

He did not appear to be bored. He was extremely attentive, in fact — and, chancing to glance at him just as he smiled down at his pretty companion with a warmth he obviously kept for his friends, Elfrida was forced to admit that a certain smile could transform a rather austere man into a very attractive heart-tumbler. Not that her heart could ever be in any danger of tumbling at a smile from him . . . heaven forbid! She did not like him in the least. But the infant he danced with seemed to like him rather too well and Elfrida wondered that her parents and friends did not warn her against encouraging the attentions of an obvious rake. Elfrida knew enough about men to recognize a dangerous womanizer when she saw one and she would not trust Luke Inskip any further than she could throw him, for her part!

She turned back to Giles who was so nice and so easy to like and so obviously to be trusted. They had spent some happy days together that week, tacitly ignoring the shadow of his brother's hostility. There was no reason why it should affect their liking for each other, their desire to be friends. Elfrida liked Giles enormously and she was aware that he liked and admired her in return. But there was no excess of sentiment in their relationship. They were simply friends who might or might not become lovers in time. For the moment their relationship made no great demands on either and that was how they liked it.

Eventually, someone drew Giles' attention to his brother, dancing with the pretty and lively Annabel. He turned to watch the couple for a few moments and, recognizing a certain

glow in Luke's eyes and the undis-
guised response it invoked, he was
annoyed. Luke ought to know better
than to expend his charm on a
susceptible girl like Annabel — and she
ought to know better than to encourage
him, silly chit!

He wondered what had brought Luke
to the club on this particular evening.
Annabel had obviously come with a
group of her friends. She loved to dance
and never lacked partners. She had
cherished a foolish yen for Luke for
some time, Giles knew — and supposed
that his brother was good-naturedly
indulging her with a little flirtation. But
it was dangerous to do so, Giles felt.
Annabel was young enough and silly
enough to make far too much of a
careless attention and end up with a
heartache. It was a little surprising that
Luke should be laying siege to an
innocent like Annabel, even to indulge
her obvious desire to be noticed by
him. Luke might often be reckless but
he was not a fool and he valued the

liking and respect of their neighbours. John Duncan, Annabel's father, would not approve of an amorous association between his daughter and a man with Luke's reputation.

Having known Annabel all her life, Giles felt a brotherly affection and concern for her and he decided to drop a quiet warning in her ear, marvelling that it was necessary when she must know that any pretty girl was at risk if she caught Luke's fickle notice. He had given her credit for more sense and attached little importance to her foolish fancy for Luke, thinking it most unlikely that his brother would ever seek to amuse himself in that quarter. Now it appeared that he had been mistaken . . .

Elfrida noticed the frown in his eyes. She touched his arm and he turned back to her. 'I hope there isn't going to be bad blood between you because of me,' she said soberly. 'I should be sorry for it.'

Relaxing, he smiled. 'Was I scowling?'

'You weren't exactly regarding him with an excess of brotherly love,' she said drily.

Giles laughed. 'Nothing to do with you,' he assured her lightly. 'Although I haven't quite forgiven him, I must admit. No, just now I dislike the way he's playing up to Annabel . . . '

'Annabel?' she queried lightly, thinking it a pretty name for a pretty girl.

'Her father farms the land that adjoins ours,' he explained. 'We've known Annabel since she was born. The Manor is virtually her second home.'

Elfrida nodded, believing she understood the situation. 'And you are very fond of her,' she said lightly.

'We all are,' he said, missing the implication. 'She looks upon us as brothers. But she's at the silly age and I suppose Luke is a very attractive man. Women seem to think so, anyway.'

'Not every woman,' Elfrida murmured, a little tartly.

'I told you that he could be very

charming when he chose,' Giles continued.

'And you think he is charming her to good effect?'

'I'm not sure. I hope she knows how to handle him, that's all. She's just a child.' There was a trace of anxiety in his tone.

Not such a child, Elfrida thought cynically. A pretty girl, however young, invariably knew how to get what she wanted and it seemed that she had Luke Inskip dancing on a string. She decided that Giles was a little jealous, perhaps without being wholly conscious of it. For Annabel was a very pretty girl . . .

6

Elfrida was not surprised when Giles excused himself from her side and was shortly seen talking to the pretty Annabel. Nor did she feel that she had been abandoned. She was the centre of an admiring group of his friends and it was simply a matter of deciding which of the many invitations to dance she wished to accept.

For the moment, she did not want to dance at all. It was a warm evening and the room was stuffy. It was also very noisy for the band had been temporarily replaced by a local pop group who believed that sound and fury could satisfactorily replace talent. Or so it seemed to the unappreciative Elfrida!

She escaped to the powder room. On her way back, she noticed an open window leading out to the terrace and she was tempted by the thought of the cool night air.

There were others on the terrace, some couples in the shadows, a group with drinks at a small table, a girl who seemed to be waiting for someone and turned eagerly as Elfrida stepped out of the window only to look away in obvious disappointment.

Elfrida walked towards the stone balustrade that bordered the terrace which overlooked a swimming pool and tennis courts and some very attractive gardens. It had once been the country house of a wealthy industrialist and it had been turned into a very successful club by a famous sportsman and some friends.

She was glad of the little breeze that cooled her hot cheeks and rippled gently through her curls. She lifted her face to the stars in appreciation of the lovely night.

Luke had also escaped from the heat and noise of the big house, needing a brief respite from Annabel's ingenuous chatter. He was smoking a cigar as he leaned on the balustrade, contemplating the dark waters of the pool and remembering midnight bathes of earlier years. He was not at all tempted despite the warmth of the night and decided wryly that old age must be overtaking him!

He became aware of the girl who stood a few feet from him when the breeze freshened and swirled the foaming layers of the flame-coloured skirt. The movement caught his eye and he turned his head to look at her, surprised to discover that she was alone. He wondered where Giles was and what he was about to neglect this very attractive girl when there were other men ready and willing to step into his shoes. Luke had not been so busy with Annabel that he had failed to notice the amount of admiring attention that his brother's new friend was attracting.

'Good evening,' he said quietly, thinking she must be aware of him.

Elfrida had not realized his presence

although she belatedly knew that she had been conscious of the faint smell of his cigar on the breeze. He stood slightly in the shadows, the moonlight only just touching the lean face and illumining the glow of his eyes. His voice startled her and she turned, stiffening, immediately on the defensive. 'Yes . . . ?' she demanded.

Luke was amused. 'I said good evening,' he said lazily. 'I'm afraid I startled you. Don't you think I'm capable of the common courtesies?'

'I've had little cause to think so to date,' she reminded him tartly, her chin lifting.

He looked at her, admiring her loveliness. 'I am not forgiven?'

'I haven't given you another thought,' she returned coldly and with very little regard for truth.

'Why should you, indeed?'

She did not reply. Luke tossed the butt of his cigar over the balustrade and watched the glowing arc of its descent until it disappeared into some bushes.

Then he looked at the girl who refused so steadfastly to look at him. He lessened the distance between them with a couple of steps in a leisurely movement. 'You seem to be enjoying yourself,' he said lightly. 'My little brother is excellent company, don't you think? Women tell me that he is a poor lover but a marvellous raconteur.'

Elfrida looked at him with quickly-sparking eyes, disliking the hint of mockery behind the words, disliking him. 'And I am told that you are the expert when it comes to telling the tale!' she said swiftly. 'No doubt the very young are so easily fooled. I am not so gullible!'

'Then I won't attempt to fool you,' he promised smoothly. He smiled down at her, the rich and very enchanting smile that had pierced so many hearts.

Elfrida was taken aback by the unexpected warmth in his smile, the usmistakably admiring glow in his grey eyes. The last thing she expected or wanted from this man was an overture of friendship. Quite immune to the good looks and the vibrant magnetism that had brought him so much success with women in the past, she turned away, meaning to return to the big house. Luke's hand closed swiftly over her wrist, compelling her to pause. Furious, her eyes blazing, she wrenched her arm from the too-confident clasp. 'What the devil are you doing?' she demanded angrily.

'Nothing so terribly that you need to lose your temper,' he said lightly. 'Don't run away. I want to talk to you.'

'I don't think we have anything to say to each other,' she said coldly, her eyes sparkling, high colour in her lovely face.

Luke caught his breath at her beauty. He did not think that he had ever known a lovelier or more exciting woman. Abruptly he realized how much he wanted her. She was intoxicating. Desire leaped fiercely and, without thinking beyond the moment, he caught her close and kissed her before she realized what he was about.

His mouth was urgent, demanding, seeking and compelling response with the touch of an expert — and Elfrida was briefly caught in the magic of the moment, her senses swimming before the onslaught of his kiss. Then, abruptly, she became aware of the fire in his passion and the strength in his embrace with all its meaningful intent — and she was alarmed. She tried to thrust him away but she seemed to have no strength against the power of the man whose arms held her so tightly that she could scarcely breathe.

She could not free herself but she told herself that she did not need to suffer his kisses. She jerked her head. 'I don't care for your brand of conversation,' she said stonily. 'I think you'd better let me go.'

Luke looked into the beautiful eyes that glowed with such anger. Feelings that did not owe their entirety to sexual need swept over him in a tidal wave. His arms tightened about her body. 'A woman like you was born to be kissed,' he said softly, urgently.

'Not by you,' she told him brutally.

He did not even flinch at the contempt in her tone. He was amused by her resistance and utterly sceptical of it for there had been instant and instinctive response in that first moment. He was too experienced to doubt that she was stirred by his sensuality whether or not she would admit it. 'But I'm a much better lover than most men,' he said, his eyes dancing.

'You're impossibly conceited!' she retorted. She wriggled a little in his embrace. 'Do you let me go or do I scream?'

He laughed. 'Kiss me first. Then I'll take you back to Giles and behave myself for the rest of the evening.'

'I don't submit to blackmail,' she said, her hands thrusting at his chest in a vain attempt to be free.

'Then I must kiss you,' he told her and suited the action to the words. He kissed her with tenderness rather than passion, surprising her and disarming her with the very unexpectedness of that gentle and oddly disturbing kiss. Quite involuntarily, all resistance melting, she relaxed against him and allowed her lips to part a little beneath the seeking sweetness of his mouth.

Excitement instantly quickened between them and she was dismayed. She stiffened so fiercely in his arms that Luke released her on the instant and was ready for the hand that flew to strike his cheek. He captured it firmly. 'No,' he said quietly.

Elfrida was almost speechless with indignation. 'You . . . you! Why, you're impossible!' she gasped. 'You kiss me against my will and I must not defend myself!'

'Where's the need? You are not under attack,' he said lightly.

'You kissed me!' she reiterated hotly, more angry with herself for enjoying it than with him for attempting it.

'An unforgettable experience,' he agreed, smiling.

Her eyes sparked. 'Not for me!'

'Next time it will be even more memorable,' he said and carried the hand that he held to his lips, pressing a light kiss into her palm and closing her fingers tightly over it.

Elfrida snatched her hand away. 'There won't be a next time,' she said, cold and hard. 'Not if you were the last man in the world!' She turned away, trembling, every line of her slender body defying him to detain her — and this time Luke allowed her to leave him.

She had not noticed the pale lemon ribbon that had fallen from her dark curls. He bent to pick it up and ran it idly through his long fingers. She was beautiful, bewitching. His blood was on fire for her. He looked down at the ribbon and knew a fierce intensity of wanting for the woman to whom it belonged. Then he tucked the ribbon away carefully in his wallet as a keepsake. It was an evening to remember . . . and she was wholly unforgettable . . .

Elfrida danced with Giles to the slow, sensual music. His cheek was lightly against her own, his arms holding her in a light embrace that reassured because it was so undemanding. Her heart warmed to him. He was so nice . . . nothing like his beast of a brother who thought that every woman who crossed his path was easy game! She was still shaken from that encounter with the man who had dared to sweep her into his arms and kiss her when she had made it very plain that she did not want his lovemaking.

Her mouth was still throbbing from the heat of his urgent lips. Her body was still bruised from the crushing strength of his arms and her tender breasts ached from the forceful contact with his powerful frame. She was still very, very angry and it took all her resolution to talk and smile and dance with Giles as though nothing had happened to upset the even tenor of the evening. But she must not spoil Giles' pleasure simply because she loathed and detested his abominable brother. She would just take the greatest possible care never to be alone with the man again even if it proved impossible to avoid him completely . . .

Giles was a little distrait himself and did not notice her tension. In fact, he was a little angry and doing his best to conceal it. He was not angry with Elfrida, of course. She was lovely, delightful, enchanting and he was glad that they were such good friends so soon. He was vexed with Annabel who had taken swift exception to his well-meant advice and had declared bluntly that she was not a child, that she could take excellent care of herself, that she was not likely to come to any harm in Luke's company and that she was tired of hearing about his much-exaggerated reputation!

It had been impossible to convince her that Luke was just as black as he had been painted in some matters. But Annabel *was* a child. She had no idea of the danger in encouraging a man who took what he wanted when he wanted without a thought for the consequences and coolly refuted responsibility when things went wrong.

Annabel had been away so much that she did not know Luke half as well as she fancied she did — and many of the scandals attaching to him had never reached her ears. She had allowed herself to picture him as a much-maligned man who only needed someone like herself to understand him, make allowances for him and reform him. As if a man like Luke could be reformed by any woman, Giles thought wryly. He had been going to the devil for much too long.

He was not Annabel's keeper . . . as she had bluntly pointed out, resenting the merest hint of criticism. But he could not help feeling concerned, a little responsible — and he knew that her father would certainly look to him to keep an eye on Annabel in the circumstances.

He supposed he had handled it badly.

Because they had been like brother and sister all their lives, he had taken too high-handed a tone to her. That was a mistake. She had dreamed of being noticed by Luke for too long in the silly way that a teenage girl did dream of someone totally unsuitable and beyond her reach — and she was not going to give up the seeming realization of a dream just for the asking. They had quarrelled and he had left her in anger and they had carefully avoided each other since — and although they would soon be friends again because they were really very fond of each other, the little spat had cast a faint shadow over the evening. He disliked to be on bad terms with anyone. It troubled him that Luke's attitude to Elfrida forced him to be cool towards his brother and now Luke's unaccountable trifling with Annabel had caused more bad feeling. It was really too bad of Luke to be so inconsiderate of the feelings of others . . .

Some of the pleasure had fled from

Annabel's evening, too. She did not know why some people had to spoil things for other people, she thought crossly. Giles ought to be pleased that she was enjoying herself if he was so fond of her. And he had no right to criticize her behaviour or her choice of escort. He ought to be more loyal to his brother, too! Annabel had particularly disliked the blunt references to Luke's rakish way of life with the implication that she would fall into his arms as readily as all the others. She was not such a fool! To get into her bed, Luke would have to marry her, she thought resolutely — and she did not think it was so impossible. Luke had a reputation, certainly. A man was expected to sow his wild oats and it made him more interesting and attractive than the callow youths of her own age. A woman liked the company and attention of an older and more experienced man. She was not going to turn down invitations simply because she was not the first woman in Luke's life! If she played her cards right, it might be that she would prove to be the last woman in his life!

Half-expecting that he would make the kind of advances that she would need to rebuff when he took her home in the early hours, Annabel did not know whether to be relieved or disappointed when he merely tilted her face with gentle fingers beneath her chin and kissed her lightly on the lips.

'Goodnight, princess,' he said with careless affection.

'But you'll come in for a nightcap, Luke? It isn't so very late,' she said, a hint of disappointment in her tone. It seemed such a let-down when she had been keyed up for an exciting if slightly dangerous interlude.

'It isn't so very early, either,' he pointed out lightly, smiling down at her. He wondered what he was about to be wasting his time with this infant when every fibre of his being quivered with the longing to hold another woman, to kiss her and make fierce, ardent love to her, to claim her for his own.

It had been a mistake to pay even brief court to Annabel. He marvelled that she had stirred him to any degree of wanting. Now he could only view her as the pretty child with the appealing ways who had always been sure of a place in his heart that owed nothing to the emotions and passions of adult loving and living.

She moved closer, invitation and eager provocation in every line of her body. 'Kiss me, Luke,' she said softly, a hint of pleading in her eyes. She raised herself on her toes to kiss his mouth.

He sighed. Then he kissed her almost savagely, seeking to whip to life the response to her youthful longing . . . and he was thankful that she was much too innocent to realize his utter lack of passion. For he would not wound her with the least implication that she was not attractive to him. She was at the sensitive age.

He kissed her because she wanted him to do so but his heart was not in it.

And Luke, always so urgent in his passions when he held a pretty woman in his arms, could only puzzle at his sudden failure to want any woman but one . . .

7

Owen Hendry did not like to be disturbed when he was working. He was struggling with a particularly difficult passage in the new book when the knocker resounded throughout the cottage. Expecting Elfrida to attend to the caller, he took no notice. The summons was repeated and Owen belatedly remembered that his daughter was out that afternoon.

He was glad she had settled down so well and made friends. It disturbed him when she wandered aimlessly about the house with little to do. It made him feel just a bit guilty about taking her away from her friends and her favourite haunts in town and bringing her to this peaceful but perhaps too uneventful corner of England.

The caller would not go away. Another assault was made on the heavy knocker. Annoyed, Owen left his papers and hurried to the door. A tall man he did not immediately recognize had his hand poised to knock again. He was certainly persistent, Owen thought irritably . . .

Luke had swiftly realized that Elfrida was keeping out of his way. She was seeing a great deal of Giles, it seemed. He could not accuse his brother of neglecting his duties about the estate. But he was certainly spending much of his time with his new girl-friend . . . and Luke was fretted by the thought of all that loveliness being wasted on his unappreciative brother. Giles was not in love with the girl. Luke knew all the signs and Giles did not evince any of them as yet. Luke was not in love with her, either. But he wanted her in a way that his gentle and undemanding brother would never understand.

He could not put her out of his mind . . . and he did not try very hard. He liked to think about her, to dwell on her beauty, her unusual eyes, her lovely skin and very kissable mouth, the seductive lines of her slender body. He wanted to see her again. He wanted to hold her again. He was tormented by the memory of her body in his arms, crushed against him, and that startled and wholly instinctive response to his kiss. He ached for her by day and dreamed of her by night. It was eight years since he had been besieged by such longing for any woman. She had bewitched him and the devil of desire was riding him hard.

The twins had met and liked Elfrida and she had been drawn so readily into their social circle that it seemed to Luke that her name was on everyone's lips wherever he went. Yet they did not meet. She apparently refused all invitations to the Manor and he suspected that she would not attend any party or any place where he was expected. He was a little amused and just a little annoyed that she should fight the inevitable. He believed she was well aware of the fierce flame which had leaped instantly to life between them. No doubt she knew of his reputation. No doubt she was very reluctant to become involved with him. No doubt she thought that he would love her and leave her with the light-hearted ruthlessness that he had brought to all his affairs in the past. No doubt she was right. But she was a fool if she thought they could defy destiny . . .

He held out his hand to her father. 'How are you? I thought it was time I called on you, welcomed you to the village.' His smile held all the considerable impact of his charm. 'Luke Inskip,' he said lightly as Owen looked blank.

'Yes, yes! Come in, my dear fellow!' Owen was a little testy, priding himself that he never forgot a face or the name that went with it. He recalled the young man perfectly well . . . had known his father years before! 'Good of you to call.' He led the way into the sitting-room.

'I hope I didn't interrupt your work

at a critical moment,' Luke said, realizing that he had called at a bad time. Elfrida was obviously not at home.

'No, no,' Owen assured him, not very convincingly. 'Fact is, the publishers are getting impatient so it's nose to the grindstone for me for a few weeks. I haven't the time I'd like to be sociable.' He waved a decanter. 'Let me give you a drink. I'd offer tea but I'm no hand at making it and Elfrida isn't in. You know my daughter, of course?'

'We have met,' Luke agreed, accepting a whiskey that he did not really want.

'She's made friends with your brother . . . young Giles. Nice lad! She's out with him now, I believe . . . making the most of the hot weather. I don't like it myself. So we're neighbours, are we? Jolly good!'

Despite his host's obvious reluctance to entertain him, Luke persevered with a rather difficult conversation until he felt the moment was ripe and then he said warmly: 'I hope you'll bring Elfrida to dinner at the Manor one evening. I know you are busy with the new book but perhaps you can spare a few hours to your friends? Just a small party, of course . . . to meet one or two people who really look forward to making the acquaintance of the celebrated Owen Hendry.'

Owen was not a social animal by nature but he was not above flattery and he could not be immune to the charm of the man. Besides, Elfrida was already on excellent terms with the Inskips and he knew it would please her if he accepted the invitation.

His mission accomplished, Luke lingered. He encouraged the writer to talk about his new book, his future commitments, the lecture tour that was in the offing — and all the while he was on edge for the slightest sound that would indicate Elfrida's return to the house. It seemed a very long time since they had met . . .

At last he was compelled to take his

leave, having persuaded his host to commit himself to a definite dinner date. The two men shook hands amicably on the doorstep just as Elfrida swung through the gate, her skin glowing from the warm sun and her eyes dancing with the aftermath of enjoyment. She looked very young and very lovely in tight-fitting scarlet jeans and matching loose tunic, her black curls dancing on her shoulders.

She had not even noticed the car parked in the road. So she was not prepared for the sight of Luke. She felt a swift clutch of dismay at her heart and checked abruptly. He smiled a greeting but she found it impossible to respond.

'Ah, my dear!' Owen greeted her with ill-concealed relief, panting to get back to his desk. 'You are in time to meet our visitor!' He turned to Luke and said expansively: 'I hope you won't rush away, after all. Elfrida will give you some tea and I'm sure you young people can entertain each other. I really must get back to my book . . .'

Without waiting for a reply, he headed for his study. Elfrida looked after him with just a hint of rue — and then turned to Luke with anger sparking in her eyes. 'I wish I was a man,' she said fiercely. 'I'd throw you out of this house!'

A little smile flickered in his eyes. 'I'm thankful that you're not a man,' he said with meaning.

She stalked past him and tossed her bag on to the sofa. He stood in the doorway, regarding her with amusement and a very real admiration. 'Do I get some tea?' he asked lightly.

'With a spoonful of cyanide in it if I had some to hand!' she snapped.

'You should be prepared for all eventualities,' he told her, amused.

'I wasn't prepared to find *you* here . . . making friends with my father to get to me! So sneaky!' she said furiously.

'Not guilty,' he said smoothly. 'I knew your father long before I met you, my lovely Elfrida.'

She rounded on him. 'Did I make you a present of my name?'

'We can scarcely stand on ceremony in the circumstances,' he said and the look in his eyes reminded her of the circumstances he had in mind.

Angry colour flaming in her face, she stalked into the kitchen and filled the kettle and began to set a tray with very bad grace.

The clash of crockery brought him to the kitchen door. 'Don't smash the china on my account,' he said lightly.

'I'd like to smash it over your head!' she retorted fierily.

'You do have a temper, my sweet. Has Giles been treated to a taste of it yet?'

'What are you doing here?' Elfrida countered. 'I don't believe that you came to see Owen if it is true that you already knew him!'

'I came to see you,' he admitted readily.

'Why? It must be obvious that I don't wish to see you!'

'Very obvious. You avoid the Manor as though the place might give you the plague . . . which makes life just a little difficult for my poor brother,' he said musingly.

'You told me that I am not welcome in your house,' she said tartly.

'Things have changed,' he told her, smiling. 'Then I didn't realize how much I want to see you in my house.'

'Want on!' she snapped, distrusting him. 'It will never happen!'

'You are a bad-tempered bitch, aren't you,' he said, amused and indulgent. The term of abuse might have been an endearment, so soft was his tone. He held out his hand to her. 'Come and be kissed, my lovely. It might sweeten your temper.'

'Go to hell!' she flared, astonished and alarmed to realize that briefly, for a moment only, she had been tempted to take him up on that offer. It was all due to that devilish smile, that little glow in his eyes that seemed to draw a woman to him even against her will.

Abruptly she lifted the latch of the back door and stepped out into the garden, leaving him. He was impossible, infuriating, she seethed. He roused her to anger in a moment . . . and she was noted for the sweetness of her temper! He was insufferable. Raging, she tightened her arms across her thudding breast and glared at the unoffending cat who stretched himself in the warm sun.

Luke touched his lips to the nape of her neck. Elfrida spun round, tingling from head to toe . . . and almost fell into the arms that were so ready to hold her. He smiled into her startled eyes and she felt a reluctant quiver of response to his undeniable attractiveness. Against her will, she was reminded of his kiss, his hard embrace, the unmistakable surging of his passion — and she knew he was about to kiss her again and something leaped within her in fierce anticipation.

Luke did not kiss her. He released her with a kind of reluctance in the way that his arms slid away from her body. She was flooded with foolish disappointment.

'I've made the tea,' he said lightly, clamping a tight rein on the passion that threatened to be his master. 'But I refuse to be mother.'

'Being father is more in your line, apparently!' Angry that he had turned from her so unexpectedly even though she did not really want him, Elfrida lashed out at him impulsively.

A flicker of annoyance darkened the grey eyes and there was a swift tightening of the lean jaw. He did not speak for a moment. Then he said quietly, a little tensely: 'You've been listening to the gossips.'

Elfrida was uncomfortable. His affairs were none of her business and it had been wrong to refer to his way of life, however rakish it might be. On the defensive, she said: 'But it's all true, isn't it . . . the things people say about you?'

'That depends on what you've heard.

Some of it is certainly true,' he said indifferently. 'I do drink too much, chase too many women and have too little regard for convention. But I pay my debts and keep on the right side of the law and I'm kind to animals and children. I'm good to my women, too . . . while they last.'

She looked at him swiftly, suspecting that he was trying to shock her. He smiled at her lazily. 'What a horrible man you are!' she said impetuously.

'But quite irresistible, don't you think?' he countered, his eyes dancing.

'And so modest!' she mocked. In recent days, meeting more people through her friendship with Giles, she had heard much about Luke Inskip and the deplorable readiness with which the women he wanted usually responded to his pursuit. It was scarcely surprising that he was so irritatingly sure of himself. But she was one woman he might pursue till he was blue in the face, she determined angrily. She was neither moved nor flattered by his obvious interest and she did not deceive herself that it owed its existence to anything but sexual attraction. It would be foolish to deny that he had a certain effect on her own emotions. But she hoped that she had too much sense to allow it to get out of hand . . .

Luke took his tea into the sitting-room and sat down in a comfortable chair, crossing one long leg over the other. Elfrida studied him with irritation. 'Do make yourself at home,' she could not resist murmuring.

He smiled, undismayed by her determination to keep him at a distance. 'I feel at home,' he said lightly. 'I know the house well, you see. As a boy I came here to have music lessons from a very old lady who was a retired concert pianist. We were great friends. More recently, I was a frequent visitor because the last tenant was a close friend . . . Angela Keith, the actress,' he added in explanation.

'Nice for you,' she said, a little stiffly. His smile deepened, teasing her gently. 'Very nice for me,' he agreed with meaning. 'It was a beautiful friendship while it lasted.'

'But, like all your 'friendships', it didn't last,' Elfrida said drily and with a hint of contempt. She was faintly disturbed to recognize a dislike of his reference to another woman. As if it mattered to her how many women he had known and lightly loved!

He shrugged. 'For the simple reason that I won't offer marriage,' he said bluntly. 'I'm not a marrying man and I make it plain at the very beginning of an affair. But I've yet to meet the woman who doesn't think I can be persuaded to change my mind.'

'I can't imagine why any woman would want to marry you,' she said tartly.

'But you don't know me very well,' he drawled, his eyes mocking her gently. 'Women are born reformers and will cling to the romantic theory that reformed rakes make the best husbands. The trouble is that I've no desire to be reformed by any woman. As for marriage with all its restraints and restrictions . . . no, not for me, thanks!'

'You weren't always so averse to the idea,' Elfrida reminded him drily.

His eyes narrowed. 'Giles has told you the story of my life, apparently.'

'Was it a secret? Shouldn't he have told me?' she demanded.

'Not to gain your sympathy on my behalf,' Luke said, brusquely.

'That wasn't the object,' she retorted. 'He felt that he ought to explain your offensive attitude.'

'I daresay it troubles him that you don't like me,' he said mockingly. 'It's quite difficult for him to remember that I'm in disgrace. He has such a forgiving nature.'

'You don't like your brother very much, do you?' she challenged, a little sharply.

He looked at her in surprise. 'I love him,' he said with sincerity. 'He is everything that I should wish to be. But I'm cast in a very different mould and it's too late to change. I've learned to live with myself. I don't expect anyone else to do so . . . least of all a woman who would only be unhappy if I married her!'

'You can't be a happy man,' Elfrida said slowly.

He raised an amused eyebrow. 'You are very naive if you believe that everyone has to be happy,' he mocked. 'Life has its moments and I take them where I can.' His grey eyes smiled at her with sudden warmth. 'Why not share a moment or two with me?' He went to her swiftly and cradled her startled face within his hands. He kissed her on the lips, very lightly but with a rare tenderness. There was something in his kiss, in his touch, that caused her heart to leap and her pulses to quicken and her body to melt with sudden longing. It was a moment of magic that took her by surprise.

He was so unexpected, so unpredictable! She put her hands to his wrists, trembling all over, marvelling at his effect on her emotions and wondering if she liked him more than she knew. Then she saw the little smile in his grey eyes and its seeming confidence, reminding her of his many conquests, was her salvation. She would not be just one more of his many women, she determined with a fierceness that surprised her.

She tugged his hands from her face and said coldly, dismissingly: 'I've better things to do with my time than spend it with you!'

Luke was disappointed and faintly disconcerted. He had come very close to giving more of himself than he wished and the rejection caused him the kind of pain he did not wish to know again. He had been near to victory, he knew. Another moment and she would have been in his arms, all doubts and fears forgotten. He wondered wryly what she had seen in his eyes to dampen the desire he was so sure that he had evoked . . .

8

Discovering that her father had accepted an invitation for them to dine with the Inskips, Elfrida's first instinct was to refuse. But Owen, usually so reluctant to become socially involved with people, seemed to be willing to give up an evening to an old acquaintance. And Elfrida could not think of any good reason to remain at home . . . certainly not when Giles was so pleased with the arrangement.

He was the first to mention the invitation that her absent-minded father had completely forgotten. He referred to it with obvious delight and relief that the antagonism between her and Luke appeared to have died down. He wished so much for her and Luke to be friends, Elfrida knew. The kind of man who was reluctant to hurt or offend anyone, swift to offer liking and friendship to everyone in the optimistic belief that it would be returned, it really distressed him that he could not speak freely of Elfrida to his slightly mocking brother or speak freely of Luke to a discouraging Elfrida.

'I think it must mean that Luke is offering the olive branch, don't you?' he said eagerly. 'You will come, Elfrida? You will try to be friends with Luke? You can't like to know that there's bad feeling between you, after all!'

'It doesn't bother me,' she said lightly. 'I can go through life quite happily, never speaking to your brother again. But I know it makes things difficult for you, Giles. So I shall come to the Manor and I'll try to be pleasant to him . . . as long as you warn him to be civil to me!'

'You started off on the wrong foot,' Giles said optimistically. 'I'm sure you'll be better friends once you give each other a chance.'

Smiling, Elfrida allowed him to indulge the hope. His heart was lighter for it, she knew. She had become very fond of Giles in a short time and she found that he was liked and respected by everyone. She soon realized what Luke had meant when he described his brother as being the kind of man he would like to be. Giles was a universal favourite. Kind, thoughtful and considerate, he was never too busy for his many friends and he liked to please, to help where he could, to make others happy and comfortable. Generous, warm-hearted, good-natured, he was the dearest of friends and the best of companions.

Elfrida felt that he was one of the nicest things that had ever happened to her. Come what may, she must not lose Giles who was a very different person to the selfish, arrogant and utterly detestable Luke Inskip. So, to please Giles, she would go to the Manor with a fairly good grace . . .

She wore a white velvet sheath that enhanced the golden tan of her skin, the tawny flecks in her eyes, the raven glossiness of her hair. Close-fitting, the dress emphasized the tautness of her breasts, the narrowness of slender waist and hips. She looked very chic, her hair worn in a gleaming plaited knob on the nape of her neck.

She took special pains to look her best, telling herself that it was for Giles who would be pleased and proud to show her off to his family and friends. But, unaccountably, it was not to Giles that she looked for approval when she arrived at the Manor.

Luke stood by the big fireplace, tall and lean and very handsome in the midnight blue dinner jacket and powder blue evening shirt, his hair gleaming like burnished gold and his rather harsh features redeemed by the smile he bestowed on the girl by his side. He turned as Elfrida and her father came into the room. Their eyes met across the room and Elfrida knew an odd little lurch of her heart.

He moved to welcome her and Owen with the smiling ease and impeccable courtesy of the perfect host. Yet there was a reserve in his manner and no real warmth in his smile as he talked to Elfrida and she knew that he was remembering their last encounter and the way she had rebuffed him. Her heart sank slightly, unaccountably, with the realization of a pride that would not allow him to risk another rebuff.

During the evening, she was favourably impressed by his efforts to ensure the success of his party and the entertainment of his guests. Without liking him any more than before, she was compelled to admit that he could be very personable. His physical attractions and his brand of charm was certainly the reason for his reputed success as a womanizer. Could any woman resist the lure of that lazy smile, the lingering warmth in those grey eyes if she had never known him at his worst? In her case, forewarned was forearmed, Elfrida thought thankfully. She was in no danger of liking him too well for peace of mind!

He did not single her out for any particular attention. That honour was kept for Annabel. She had heard that the girl was his newest flirt and that they were constantly together. There were rumours that he was planning to settle down at last. There was a certain amount of speculation that he had always intended to marry the girl whose father's land ran side by side with his own. Elfrida did not know him well enough to judge how fond he was of the girl or if he had any thought of marriage. He was certainly very attentive to Annabel that evening. To her, he was pleasant, courteous, even friendly but there was not the slightest hint that he found her attractive or cherished hopes of a light-hearted affair with her. The way he had looked, the way he had spoken, the way he had kissed her might have been a figment of her imagination, she thought wryly.

Of course, she was relieved that he had accepted her dismissal. She had not been at all flattered by his pursuit. She had not attained the grand old age of twenty-two without being well aware of the impact of her physical attractions on a man. But most men, in her experience, had the grace to behave as though they were motivated by more than mere sexual interest. Luke Inskip was too direct for her taste, she decided . . . and refused to wonder if she would have been as willing as all the other women in his life if he had pretended to a few finer feelings . . .

Giles had been a little anxious that evening. He knew that Luke could charm the birds from the treetops if he chose and he feared that Elfrida's loveliness might yet find its way to his brother's interest. She might laughingly dismiss the flirtatious approaches of the other men who attempted to woo her away from him, including Guy and Simon, but it seemed to him that no woman laughed when Luke turned his roving eye towards her.

But he soon realized that he had nothing to fear in that direction. He might be surprised that his amorous brother seemed so indifferent to a girl as beautiful and as exciting as Elfrida but he could only be relieved. Luke made no attempt to charm Elfrida. He was courteous but distant. Annabel took most of his attention. Giles could not approve of that rapidly ripening affair but he felt he could relax his vigilant eye on this particular occasion for Luke would not overstep the mark while the Colonel was breathing down his neck. So Giles was free to devote himself to Elfrida and to enjoy the evening.

Annabel, too, had steeled herself for the evening. She was thrilled that Luke was living up to all her expectations but it was so unlikely that she could hold a man like him for very long that she had expected to be neglected for the more mature and undeniably beautiful new-comer. She had noticed a sudden stiffening of his tall frame and a very odd expression in his grey eyes when Elfrida Hendry arrived. But it had flown in a moment and there had been no further indication that he felt any particular interest in the woman, much to Annabel's relief.

She knew herself to be utterly cast into the shade by Elfrida. It was to her credit that she did not resent it. Instead she felt interest in the girl who had become so important so swiftly to Giles who was not an accomplished flirt like his brothers.

Giles was something special in Annabel's life. Fairly close in age, they had always been good friends and constant companions throughout childhood and adolescence. She valued him even while she took him very much for granted. He was neglecting her lately because his time and attention were taken up by Elfrida but he had always been more brother than friend and Annabel was not silly enough to be jealous. She had always known that one day she would take second place in his affections. But she was concerned for his happiness. She did not think that

Elfrida Hendry was right for Giles. She was a little too sophisticated, a little too worldly, a little too light of heart for someone as loving and giving as Giles. She could not have known another man like him, Annabel felt on a surge of affection. The Giles of this world were few and far between and much too good for someone like Elfrida who would not really appreciate him!

Luke responded to the light chatter of the women and the more serious conversation of the men and he scarcely glanced at Elfrida as she talked and laughed with his attentive brothers. But he was very conscious of her even while he played the part of dutiful host.

He had not seen her since that day at the cottage, almost a week ago. He had not wished to see her for he had been annoyed and more hurt than he cared to admit by the woman who had thrust him away so coldly, so contemptuously. He had tried to put her out of his mind, spending far more time than was wise with Annabel in the effort to convince himself that he no longer wanted a woman who so obviously did not want him. But she had proved impossible to forget. She was almost an obsession, haunting his days and his nights with the image of her beautiful face and bewitching body.

His heart had somersaulted when she walked into the room that evening. So lovely in that stunning gown, starkly white against the bronzed skin and the gleaming jet of her hair. He had never known a lovelier woman . . . or wanted any woman so much, he admitted wryly. He wanted to make urgent and demanding love to her, sweep her to the heights of passion, carry her over the threshold of ecstasy. But, more than anything, he wanted to humble the woman who denied him friendship even while she took his brothers to her heart . . .

Giles took Elfrida on a brief tour of the beautiful old house. When they returned, he was swept away by Annabel who demanded that his reliable memory of a past occasion should settle an argument she was having with Simon.

Elfrida, smiling, turned to the open window and stepped out to the paved terrace, meaning to explore the sunken rose garden on her own. It was one of those glorious summer evenings when the air was still and warm and heavy with the scent of sun-kissed flowers.

She wandered along a path, admiring a rose here and touching a reverent finger to a rose there, enjoying the beauty of her surroundings and feeling just a twinge of envy of the Inskips who owned the Manor and its many acres. This was more than a landed estate or a country house, she thought with genuine admiration. It was a home, much-loved and carefully-tended. She had never known a real home, having travelled the world with her father since early childhood. She had no roots such as the Inskips had put down, generations before, when they established themselves and the Manor in the little village of Frisby.

'It's a pleasant place on an evening like this,' Luke said quietly.

Elfrida turned slowly. She had known he stood behind her even before he spoke. She had not heard his approach and yet she had been aware of his presence in the very fibres of her being. She smiled at him ... and it was perhaps the first time she had allowed any real warmth to touch her eyes or her voice when dealing with him. 'It's beautiful,' she agreed. 'So peaceful ... the world seems a million miles away.'

'My mother created this garden. Roses were her special love,' he explained. 'She needed a quiet corner at times with four boisterous boys to plague her,' he added with a little smile.

Elfrida liked him in that moment. There was something very tender, very warm, in the way that he spoke of his dead mother. Having never known her own mother who had died in childbirth, she had always envied the

140

special relationship that existed between mother and child. She felt that the relationship of Luke and his mother had been very special — and remembered that he was the first-born. 'I wish I had known her,' she said truthfully. 'Giles has been showing me the house and I was fascinated by the family portraits. You are most like your mother, I think.'

'In more ways than one,' he said drily. 'She was not very popular, being one to speak her mind without fear or favour and to go her own way with little regard for convention or public opinion. So you've had the grand tour? I hope you weren't too bored. Giles has all the history of the place at his finger-tips and forgets that not everyone shares his enthusiasm for old houses.'

'It's beautiful and I wasn't at all bored,' she said swiftly.

'My house is honoured by your approval,' he murmured, a little smile lurking in his eyes.

Elfrida stiffened, suspecting mockery.

She looked at him coldly, abruptly reminded of her last visit to the Manor, disliking him all over again. 'Only regard for your brother brought me over its threshold this evening!' she said tartly.

'So I imagine. I appreciate the cost to your pride,' he said lightly. 'May we now forget a regrettable misunderstanding? I am doing my best to make amends, you know.' He held out his hand to her. 'Cry pax?' He had meant to treat her with a coolness that conveyed the death of his interest. Yet she was too lovely to be ignored and he wanted her too much to miss the smallest opportunity to improve on their relationship.

Elfrida regarded him doubtfully. She did not trust him in the slightest. She would not be at all surprised if he swept her into his arms without warning and forced his kisses on her reluctant lips once more. Yet, meeting his eyes, she could not discern any hint of such an intent. He was looking down at her with something very like friendliness in his grey eyes . . . and she could not help feeling that she did not deserve such generosity in view of the way she had rebuffed him at their last meeting.

He took her hand and she did not pull it away. He stood very close, smiling down at her. He was too close for comfort, Elfrida decided, much too aware of him. The sensuality of the man seemed to stir a most unwelcome response in her slender body with the merest touch of his hand. She tingled all over with an excitement she did not wish to know. She was furious with the heart that quickened at his nearness. 'Very well,' she agreed, almost reluctantly, wondering if it was wise to encourage him at all. Suddenly suspecting that he would take immediate advantage of a momentary weakness, she added hastily: 'For Giles' sake.'

His eyes hardened. 'We must not disappoint Giles, of course,' he said with a faintly mocking smile. He was hurt by her inability to like him for his own sake and he was angry with himself for inviting another rebuff. She simply did not mean to give him a chance to convince her that he was not as contemptible as his behaviour to date had led her to believe, he thought wryly, a little impatiently. He wondered why it mattered. There were more than enough willing women in the world. So why should he waste time and energy on wanting this one who so obviously did not want him?

As if on cue, Annabel came out to the terrace and called to him. He left Elfrida with a murmur of excuse and she watched him join the girl and slip an arm about her shoulders. Annabel looked up at him in obvious adoration and Elfrida knew a sharp little tug of something that might almost be jealousy. They were on the very best of terms. They had known each other for years and he was undoubtedly fond of her. Perhaps lifelong affection had turned to loving. Probably Annabel was the kind of woman to suit Luke

. . . loving, trusting, never questioning, asking little of him and always devoting herself to his happiness. But did he mean to marry her? He had declared that he was not a marrying man . . .

9

Giles came in search of Elfrida some minutes later. She had not followed Luke back to the house, needing a few moments to overcome an odd little depression. She had been faintly piqued by the ease with which he had turned from her and the eagerness with which he had hastened to join Annabel. He was an enigma, she thought crossly . . . and not at all to be trusted! One could surely never know what prompted him to those occasional offers of the olive branch . . . and it was a little humiliating to feel that it was nothing more than fleeting sexual attraction.

She supposed she was just another woman to Luke Inskip and there had been too many women in his life by all accounts! No doubt he only wanted her because she refused to want him. She was something of a challenge but he rapidly lost interest when she rebuffed him. She was thankful. His careless contempt for all women must make it quite impossible for her to think well of him.

But she could not help feeling that if his nature had been as attractive and as appealing as the smile that occasionally warmed his eyes, it might have been much too easy for her to respond to him as other women did . . .

She turned to Giles with smiling warmth for his pleasant personality would soon soothe her ruffled feathers, she knew. She brushed aside his apology for neglecting her, assuring him that she had enjoyed her exploration of the gardens. 'You have a lovely home,' she said with a hint of wistful envy.

'I hope you'll say something of that kind to Luke,' he said, smiling. 'He has a very deep feeling for the Manor and I know it will please him.'

'I've just been talking to him,' Elfrida told him lightly. 'He was very pleasant, quite on his best behaviour!'

'I'm glad,' Giles said simply. 'It's been a nice evening, hasn't it? I think you have enjoyed it?'

'Very much,' she said lightly, smiling with affectionate warmth. 'I like the Duncans. And I'm enchanted with the twins. I could easily fall for Guy — or is it Simon? All I have to do is learn to tell them apart!'

'You aren't safe with either of them,' he warned her, his eyes dancing. 'Stick with me, Elfrida. I'll take good care of you.' And he bent his head to brush her lips lightly with his own.

Elfrida touched her hand to his cheek on a surge of tenderness. It was a little loving gesture that went directly to his heart. 'You are so nice,' she said warmly. 'I do love you.'

The impulsive words were uttered from the heart but they did not hold the meaning, the depth of commitment, that such words should. She regretted them almost before they left her lips for the look in his grey eyes smote her with a sudden realization of their importance to him.

Giles caught her to him, holding her very close. She could hear the heavy pounding of his heart. With an odd sensation of waters closing over her head, she heard the little catch of his breath before his arms tightened fiercely about her and his lips sought her own with swift hunger.

It was the first time that their relationship had passed beyond the bounds of friendship. It was the first time that they had kissed as lovers.

Elfrida was not sure how much it meant to Giles . . . too much, she feared, knowing that it meant little to her. His embrace, his kiss, his murmured endearments could not stir the smallest response. He was her very good friend and she loved him dearly. But this abrupt change in their relationship, born of her impulsive words, was not what she had wanted to happen. But she could not hurt the man who had been so very good to her and asked so little of her . . . it seemed too cruel, too cold-blooded to tell him that loving him was impossible for her. She had no reason to be so sure. He was the kind of man that any woman would want and she ought to love him — and perhaps real loving was quiet and gentle and undemanding and the fierce excitement that his brother could evoke so easily was a longing that could only lead to heartache . . .

Whistling Dolittle's famous song from *My Fair Lady*, Giles ran down the wide staircase to join his brothers at breakfast the following morning.

The sun was shining and the sky was very blue and all was right with his world. He did not question his new-found happiness. He simply knew that it was all due to Elfrida and he did not doubt that she felt just as he did on this bright morning. He had found all the assurance that a man could want in the warmth of her lips and the melting surrender of her slender body to his embrace.

They had been friends. Suddenly, all in a moment, they had become lovers and Giles knew it was right and natural and destined. He knew they would marry because it was the inevitable ending to their love story. But it was early days and he was content to love and be loved and enjoy the new and wonderful world that he had found with Elfrida.

'*I'm getting married in the morning . . .* ' he sang blithely, in excellent voice. '*Get me to the church . . . get me to the church* — good morning! How are our hangovers this morning?' He pulled a chair from the table and sat down, beaming on his brothers.

From behind a newspaper, Guy waved a piece of toast in casual greeting. 'Is the child trying to tell us something?' he demanded drily of nobody in particular.

Simon swallowed the last of his coffee and rose from the table with the day's work in mind. 'The lad's in love,' he said indulgently, slapping Giles on the shoulder as he passed his chair.

Luke looked up from the letter that did not appear to please him for there was a scowl in the grey eyes and a certain grimness about his mouth. 'You're full of bonhomie this morning,' he commented suspiciously.

Giles, on the best of terms with all the world that morning, smiled on him with brotherly affection. 'Why not? It's a grand morning — a beautiful morning!'

'Oh lord!' Guy groaned in mock dismay. 'Don't encourage him to burst into song again or we shall have the whole of *Oklahoma* over bacon and eggs!'

Giles grinned, unabashed.

Luke looked at him intently. Then he returned to his letter. But the words held no meaning for him. There was a strange, sick dismay about his heart. Giles was a fool, he thought wearily. Oh, not for falling in love. That happened to the best of men! But for thinking that Elfrida was right for him or that he could make her happy. She needed a strong, sensual man to match fire with fire. Giles was too gentle, too kindly, too sensitive. They were totally unsuited to each other!

For once in his life, Luke was at a loss. If he tried to intervene, to caution, to advise, he would incur his brother's resentment and inevitably be accused of wanting Elfrida for himself. And that was a charge he was in no position to deny, he thought ruefully.

He had scarcely slept for thinking of her, for wanting her. And he made up his mind to humble his pride and seek her out that very day. For she must be made to admit that something had sparked between them that could not be ignored! Now, judging by his brother's mood of elation, it was too late. Some step had been taken or some threshold had been crossed, obviously. For Giles was dancing on air! It did not take much intelligence to work out that only Elfrida could be responsible.

What to do? He could not prevent

Giles from loving and yet he knew beyond a shadow of doubt that his brother was heading for heartache. Elfrida did not love him and Luke was convinced that she never would. He was desperately anxious for Giles. His own life had been marred by the loss of the woman he hoped to marry and he did not want that kind of suffering for Giles. But how to protect him?

'Problems . . . ?' Giles demanded cheerfully, liberally applying marmalade to toast.

Luke folded the letter. 'Nothing that can't be solved,' he said, a little grimly, determined to find a way to avert disaster for Giles, refusing to believe that his concern was dictated by the tug of his own interests.

'Anything I can do?' Giles volunteered.

A wry smile flickered in Luke's eyes. The one thing he might ask of his brother was certainly the one thing he would refuse — to give up the girl who seemed to be persuading his cautious heart into loving. 'No . . . ' He poured fresh coffee into his cup and sat back, regarding Giles with thoughtful eyes. 'It appears that the evening was a resounding success from your point of view,' he said lightly. 'I hope I am restored to your good books. I trust you noticed that I went out of my way to be pleasant to your Elfrida.'

'It was a great evening,' Giles said warmly, reverting readily to the subject that was nearest and dearest to his heart. 'Certainly I noticed — and I'm grateful! I'm glad that you seem to be liking each other a little better at last. She's a grand girl, Luke!'

'Too good for you,' Guy declared with brotherly candour, lowering the newspaper to wink at Luke. 'Why don't you do the decent thing and stand aside to let a real man get to her . . . meaning myself, of course?'

'I'm all the man she needs,' Giles returned confidently and a little smile hovered about his lips as he recalled the kisses that had set a new seal on their relationship and his heart lifted anew at the recollection that she had said she loved him. He loved her, he knew . . . much, much more than she could ever know. She was a wonderful girl and he was the luckiest man in the world!

Luke knew an instinctive dislike of the implication of that smile, the glow of triumph in his brother's eyes. He had not supposed the affair to have progressed to the point of intimacy. Now he wondered. Giles was no celibate, after all — and he thought it very likely that Elfrida would respond readily to the desire of a man that she obviously liked. It angered him suddenly and sharply to think of her in his brother's arms, pliant and willing. He was shaken with a fury, that was abruptly directed against a girl who might be as wanton as all the others for all her pretence of outrage when he had dared to kiss her too demandingly.

'Don't rush to the altar,' he said lightly but with a faint edge to his tone. 'You scarcely know the girl and a woman always lies to her lovers.' He pushed away his untouched coffee and rose — just as Giles, fists clenching in swift anger, leaped to his feet to confront him.

'What the devil do you mean by that remark?' he demanded furiously.

Luke smiled. But there was a flicker of regret for the hostility that Giles felt so quickly towards him of late . . . and all due to Elfrida. 'Very little,' he drawled reassuringly. 'I'm simply advising you not to rush into anything.' He brushed past his brother, leaving him angry and baffled.

'Don't be such a hothead,' Guy said carelessly. 'Luke only says that kind of thing to get you going. It doesn't mean anything.'

'I'm not so sure,' Giles returned, torn between a desire to have it out with Luke and a feeling that it might be wiser to let well alone.

'Don't let him needle you. He doesn't like it because you got to Elfrida before he did,' Guy said sagely.

Giles turned to look at him, frowning. 'He isn't interested in her, I'm thankful to say!'

Guy laughed. 'Any girl who looks like that interests him,' he declared drily. 'She interests me, too. But she only has eyes for you, it seems. You're a lucky devil! Our Luke doesn't waste time on lost causes. But don't think he likes it because he doesn't.'

'I think you're mistaken,' Giles said, a little doubtfully, trying not to remember small incidents that might lead him to the conclusion that there was something in Guy's words.

Guy shrugged. 'Please yourself.' He did not mean to argue. He had his own opinion of the situation.

Giles sat down to finish his breakfast. But his appetite had fled and a vague shadow was cast over the brightness of the morning. But he was not downcast for long. Whatever Luke might feel about Elfrida, he knew that she had little liking or admiration for him. She might make the effort to be pleasant to

158

him as she had certainly done on the previous evening. But it was an effort. She did not like Luke at all and in view of the way he had treated her, it was not surprising. Thinking things over in the light of his knowledge of their clashes, it seemed ludicrous to Giles that there could be the slightest degree of attraction on either side. He decided to dismiss Guy's comments from his mind. It was always possible that Guy was just a little jealous of Elfrida's obvious preference for him and was trying to stir up trouble . . .

Later that morning, he was on the point of riding with Elfrida across the fields to Lethaby's Farm when Barney came hurrying to call him to the telephone. He dismounted and left her with a promise of a swift return.

The mare was fidgetty and Elfrida, an experienced horsewoman, recognized that she was sensitive to a stranger on her back. She talked gently and soothingly and walked her up and down while she waited for Giles.

Luke rounded the corner of the stables and reined his black stallion abruptly as he saw Elfrida on the chestnut mare, slim and lovely in jodhpurs and bright yellow sweater, her black hair tied back from her face.

Hearing hooves on the cobbles of the stable yard, Elfrida turned her head. Luke nudged Nimrod forward with his knees. Meeting the grey eyes that seemed to regard her without warmth, Elfrida felt a little uncomfortable. It was all very well for Giles to declare that his brother would be happy for her to ride the mare. Giles was an incurable optimist. Luke loved his horses and guarded them jealously and she could not help feeling that it might have been wiser to ask if she might ride the chestnut horse. But it was not the easiest thing in the world to approach him, she thought wryly.

Luke realized that she was on the defensive — and he knew why. He was sorry that she had such a poor opinion of him that she could suppose he would resent her use of one of his horses. He was pleased to give her pleasure.

The mare was restless and he noticed with swift approval that Elfrida's seat and hands were excellent and that she obviously knew just how to handle a highly-strung animal. 'I'm glad to see you on Santana,' he said lightly in greeting, swinging himself from the saddle and tossing the rein to a hovering groom. 'She doesn't get enough exercise and she's getting fat and lazy.' He strolled over to run his hand lightly down the mare's neck and she nudged him with her long nose in obvious affection.

Elfrida was surprised into warming to him. He would have been perfectly justified in showing annoyance, she felt. 'Giles felt you wouldn't mind . . . ' she began with a hint of apology in her tone.

'I don't,' he said. 'Giles knows me very much better than you do.' He looked at her with a little smile in his eyes. 'Do you ride alone? She can be temperamental as you've already seen.'

161

'I'm waiting for Giles. He's talking on the telephone,' she explained. 'We're going to visit one of the farms — on estate business, of course. I'm not encouraging him to neglect his work.'

His smile deepened. 'You couldn't do so,' he said confidently. 'Giles knows that I rely on him and he would never let me down.'

There was very real affection and trust in his tone and something in his smile that unexpectedly caused Elfrida's heart to contract. It suddenly occurred to her that she would like him to speak of her in just that way and with just that particular warmth in his grey eyes . . . but it would never be. Because it was due to loving . . . the very real love he obviously knew for his young brother. Looking down at him, she had a brief glimpse of the man he must have been before tragedy struck and took his love and left him apparently incapable of loving again . . . and there was an inexplicable heaviness about her heart . . .

10

They talked for a few moments, idly, in unexpected amity, touching on everything but the personal. He stood beside the mare, his hand lightly resting on Santana's neck, golden hairs glinting in the bright sun and the long, strong fingers gently teasing the coarse mane. His smile was warm and friendly, crinkling his eyes and redeeming the slight harshness of his features. Perhaps he was only making the effort to be pleasant in order to please Giles but it made everything much more comfortable, Elfrida decided thankfully.

Yet she was not entirely at her ease with him. He was much too attractive for any woman's peace of mind, she thought ruefully. She was constantly on her guard against the feelings he could evoke so easily. She wondered wryly if she would like him better if she did not always have to fight his undeniable effect on her emotions.

Inevitably she compared him with Giles who did not make such fierce demands on her . . . and decided that she preferred the more restful relationship. She refused to wonder if Giles was not just a little dull. A man like Luke might be exciting but he was much too elusive. There was a need within her for a permanent and settled relationship that would lead to marriage and the kind of home that she had never known. She did not doubt that Giles could and would provide her with both. But there was not the faintest hope of finding them with Luke who was not a marrying man by his own declaration. He was very attractive but he was not a man that it would be wise to love — and Elfrida could only be thankful that her heart was not at risk!

Even while they talked, Luke wondered if there was any easy way to caution her against allowing Giles to become too attached to her. A woman could always dissuade a man from loving her if she chose . . . and Elfrida must have had plenty of that kind of experience. She was a beautiful and very desirable woman and there must have been other men who found it easy to love her.

It was ironic that he and Giles, the brother who meant so much to him, should want the same woman. He could take her and forget her as he had taken and forgotten other women in the past. But Giles would probably commit himself wholeheartedly to loving and suffer for it! A check on his emotions before they got out of hand might spare him a great deal of pain. Elfrida could do it — but would she? Luke fancied that she meant to have Giles . . . and wondered if she was blind or merely indifferent to the truth that she could have him for the lift of a finger!

He was tormented with longing. Wanting her was a weakness that he was unable to master for all the trying. She was lovely, enchanting — and he was bewitched, he thought ruefully. But Giles stood in his way and he could not thrust his own brother aside to gain what he wanted . . .

Giles was delayed by the need to make another call as a result of his conversation with one of the tenant farmers. He sent an apologetic message to Elfrida via Barney. She did not mind waiting but she was finding it something of a strain to spend so long in Luke's company. He was being too nice, she thought wryly. She was safer when they were at loggerheads!

As Barney went back to his work, Luke said quietly: 'You're spending much of your time with Giles. Do you think it's wise to encourage him so much? He's falling in love with you, Elfrida. I wish you would put an end to it before he gets hurt.'

Colour flooded her face. She looked away from the directness of his grey eyes that caused her heart to flutter so oddly. Luke's concern was entirely for his brother, she told herself firmly. It would be foolish to suppose that he could be motivated by a desire to whisk her out of Giles' arms and into his own. She did not believe his interest in her was deep or lasting and there was no future in getting involved with a man like Luke even if opportunity offered.

'He won't be hurt,' she said stiffly even as she wondered if it was avoidable. Luke was right, of course. Giles *was* falling in love and she did not know how to dissuade him. She did not want to lose him but she did not want him to love her, she thought with a twinge of conscience for the encouragement she had already given.

Luke gestured impatiently. 'But you don't care for him,' he said, very sure. She might be fond of Giles but she was certainly not in love with him!

'I won't hurt him,' she repeated. 'I care more than you think.' Resenting his easy assumption that he knew her feelings very much better than she did, she was prepared to exaggerate her affection for Giles rather than give Luke the slightest cause to suppose that *he* mattered to her!

'Not enough and not in the right way,' Luke said firmly. 'Put an end to it!'

Her chin tilted. He was infuriatingly sure of himself . . . and damnably arrogant. Did he really suppose she would meekly do as he said simply because he said it! 'Not at your bidding,' she retorted with a cool little smile.

'You do know how he feels about you, I suppose?' Luke demanded, struggling with the anger that soared at her seeming indifference to the hurt she would certainly inflict on an unsuspecting and much too generous heart.

'Oh, I'm not completely insensitive,' Elfrida said airily.

'Pleases you, does it?' he said on a sudden spurt of anger. 'Boosts your ego?'

Her eyes flashed. 'I don't collect men the way you collect women!'

He was heartened by the hint of

resentment behind the words. She did not like his reputation, apparently. The resistance he sensed in her was due to a determination that she would not become just one more name on the list of his conquests.

'At least I am honest with my women,' he drawled, amusement glinting in his eyes. 'I always play fair.'

She looked at him with dislike. Her voice shook slightly as she said with feeling: 'The more I see of you the more I dislike you!'

Luke laughed. 'But you promised Giles that you would be friends with me — and surely you will go to any lengths to please Giles?' he said mockingly.

'We'll never be friends!' she said fiercely.

'I believe you are right,' he agreed lightly, smiling. 'Lovers, perhaps . . . '

Elfrida stiffened with shock and anger. 'Never!' Santana tossed her head in nervous reaction to the sharp tone and Elfrida patted her soothingly. 'Stand away!' she commanded Luke impatiently. 'You make her nervous!'

'Nonsense! She doesn't care for the way you speak to me,' he returned lightly. 'She loves me, you see.' He put an arm over the mare's neck and murmured something in her ear. Santana gave a soft whinny and nudged him with affection. Luke made a show of surprise as he produced a small apple from the pocket of his hacking jacket.

It was astonishing and a little alarming that she could be so furious with him at one moment and warm to him so suddenly the next. It was the occasional glimpse of a tenderness beneath the harsh, uncaring exterior that threatened her resolution not to like him too much for peace of mind . . .

'I'm going to hurry Giles,' she said abruptly. 'We ought not to keep the horses standing so long.'

Luke caught her as she dropped to the ground from the saddle, his hands lightly encircling her waist. She looked at him swiftly, suspiciously — and her heart gave an odd little lurch at the glow in his eyes. 'Let me go, Luke,' she said shakily, discovering that he could still flood her with quivering excitement at the merest touch. Woman-like, she knew instinctively that the wanting was equally fierce in him. But, woman-like, she was bound to resist a physical force that owed nothing to mutual liking. She could not, would not surrender to mere desire for a man she did not even like very much!

She was trembling. Luke, the experienced lover, the confident conqueror, interpreted her reaction as revulsion. Dismayed, he released her. He wanted her desperately but he could not force himself on a woman who did not want him and it seemed that he had lost all his powers of persuasion. She did not find him attractive or even worthy of liking — and there was an end to it, he thought grimly.

Giles came hurrying at that moment, knowing he had kept Elfrida waiting much too long. From a distance there was nothing in the little tableau to disturb him. And Elfrida greeted him so warmly that it was not surprising that he should suppose it to be evidence of affection rather than relief at his timely arrival.

Luke did not wait to see them off on their ride. With a compression of his lips and something that defied analysis in his eyes, he turned away.

Elfrida watched him go and suddenly all her pleasure in the proposed expedition seemed to evaporate. She loved to ride and she had been looking forward to a canter over the fields with Giles at her side. But her heart seemed to sink as Luke walked off without a friendly word or a backward glance.

She had the oddest conviction that she had hurt him . . . but that would imply that he cared sufficiently to mind her persistent refusal of his advances. He did not, of course. He was merely the kind of man who did not like to be denied and Elfrida knew, with a little

172

flurry of excitement about her heart, that Luke wanted her very much. But only a fool would give way to the feelings that he aroused for she also knew, resenting the knowledge, that his desire for her had nothing to do with love. He was a very different man to his brother . . .

Giles became more dear to her with every passing day. They were friends and companions rather than lovers. Elfrida knew that he assumed a depth of feeling on her part that did not exist but it seemed too cruel, too cold-blooded to declare that she could never love him as he apparently loved her — and how could she be sure? Perhaps her affection for him was as near to loving as she would ever get. Perhaps the kind of loving she expected to feel only existed in the minds of romantic novelists, she thought wryly. Perhaps she could be very happy with Giles who would never give her a moment's disquiet and would be a loyal and loving husband to the end of his life.

What woman could ask for more?

She knew, of course. She knew exactly what was missing from their relationship and it was a disturbing lack. Giles was not a sensual man and his lovemaking was gentle, undemanding, without the passion that might have stirred her to response. It was all very well to feel that things would be different if she married him. She knew in her heart that it would be a mistake. Sex might not be the be-all and end-all of marriage but it played a very vital part. At the same time, she found it impossible to tell Giles that she did not want him as a woman ought to want the man she was thinking of marrying. Perhaps she attached too much importance to the kind of excitement and yearning that his brother could evoke too easily for it could never be as enduring or as precious as the kind of loving that Giles offered. A moment of magic could not be compared with a lifetime of loving.

So they drifted on the gentle tide of

mutual affection and liking for each other's company and Elfrida said nothing to contradict the rapidly-growing belief among Giles' family and friends that they meant to marry. And she kept out of Luke's way as much as possible.

Inevitably they met from time to time. Inevitably the age-old tension existed between them and Elfrida wondered why the very air seemed to throb with the electricity of their mutual attraction whenever they were together, however briefly. She continued to fight it. It was a weakness that she despised . . . and her growing commitment to Giles made it more and more impossible to surrender to the rakish attractions of his brother.

His affair with Annabel seemed to be thriving but he refused to be drawn when family or friends hinted at his plans. And because he was obviously not a marrying man, they soon tired of teasing him. Annabel persisted in hoping that he would marry her but she did not try to lure him into an engagement. Sensibly, she was content to be the current woman in his life — and she kept him sufficiently at arms length to spur him to thoughts of marriage. She was too inexperienced to appreciate that his failure to alarm her with too much ardour stemmed from lack of interest rather than gentlemanly instincts — and Luke was too sensitive to her feelings to emphasize his indifference.

For the time being, it suited him to dance attendance on the pretty Annabel. She made few demands on him and he did not wish to become too involved just now, however lightly, with any woman other than the one who still kept him captive. He had meant to forget his longing for Elfrida but it had proved impossible. He had meant to conquer the desire for his brother's love but it grew fiercer with every day that passed. Perhaps he might have forced her from his mind and his blood if he had been convinced that she loved

Giles. But he did not think that she did.

It seemed to him that she hid her real feelings under a cloak of caring for Giles. But she would not marry Giles in cold blood. She was not that kind of woman. He could be patient. She was worth all the waiting. He was sure that she felt desire as he did. He was sure that she ached for him as he ached for her. But she was proud and stubborn and he had handled their relationship badly, unaware that she would become so important to him. However, he refused to accept that he had damaged his chances beyond repair.

He set out to redeem himself . . .

When they met, he was pleasant, friendly, courteous — but not so charming that she could be suspicious. He did not go out of his way to contrive meetings although there were days when the need for her was almost too great for comfort. He was careful not to disturb her with any hint of his feelings. He did not try to make love to her with eyes or smile or speech. He deliberately implied acceptance of her preference for Giles and he made it clear that he did not mean to embarrass her with his attentions. He gradually overcame her defensive attitude. He gently encouraged her to think more kindly of him, to feel that she might have been hasty in judging him so harshly. They did not become friends, exactly — but antagonism no longer existed. Occasionally she relaxed sufficiently to smile at him with a warmth that took him by surprise, caught unexpectedly at his heart and he was shaken with a flood of longing.

His physical attractions and the famous Inskip charm had always won him any woman he wanted. He liked women but, all unconsciously, he had begun to regard every one he met as an easy conquest. It was a salutary lesson to discover that Elfrida was not so easily won. He took a long, analytical look at himself and did not care for what he saw. He had become arrogant, over-confident, too careless in his dealings with people. He had supposed that he did not need to make the slightest effort to endear himself to others. He had become insufferably conceited, in fact — just as Elfrida had once declared, he recalled wryly. He had been too proud, firmly convinced that the woman did not exist who could bring him to his knees with wanting. But Elfrida had humbled him. Now pride did not seem to matter. He wanted her at any cost . . . more than he had wanted any woman since Sybil.

But she continued to encourage Giles to love her and to encourage everyone else to believe that she meant to marry him.

And Luke, wanting her desperately and getting nowhere for all his efforts, began to feel that he could not blame any woman who chose his gentle, thoughtful, caring brother in preference to someone like himself who had a well-earned reputation for rough, tough living and loving . . .

11

It was market day in Melling and the country town was busy and bustling. The narrow pavements were crowded and tempers were fraying slightly in the heat of the afternoon. It was one of those rare summers when the sun shone day after day, a golden orb in a clear blue sky, and people were beginning to sigh for a break in the weather.

Elfrida came out of a shop with her arms full of packages, her bag swinging from her shoulder. She caught a glimpse of a bus just disappearing round a corner. There would be a wait of nearly an hour before the next one, she knew, and it was certain to be too crowded for comfort.

She sighed. It had seemed like a good idea to catch up on some shopping but she was rapidly regretting the impulse that had brought her into Melling that afternoon. Giles was busy with the builders who were working on necessary repairs to some of the farm cottages. Owen was endeavouring to finish the final chapter of his book. Elfrida, unusually left to her own devices, had donned a cool cotton frock and summer sandals and caught the bus into Melling. Her small car was in the local garage, having a new clutch fitted, and it had seemed almost an adventure to travel by public transport.

She was hot and tired and thirsty. She looked around for a café where she might dawdle over a cup of tea and a cake until her bus was due. She waited on the edge of the pavement for a pause in the constant flow of traffic down the narrow High Street . . . and turned, startled, at a touch on her arm.

Luke had espied her from the distance and quickened his steps to catch her before she disappeared into the crowd. Now he smiled down at her surprised face. 'This is unexpected,' he said lightly. 'Let me take some of those parcels.'

She relinquished them immediately. 'I wish I'd known you were coming to Melling,' she said. 'I might have cadged a lift.'

He raised an eyebrow. 'No car?'

'Didn't Giles mention it? It's in the garage for new clutch plates. I came in by bus.'

'I can certainly take you back,' he offered. 'Whenever you're ready ... ' He did not give a second thought to the business appointment which had brought him to Melling that afternoon. It was quite unimportant compared to her need of him, however trivial.

'Would you? I'd be grateful,' Elfrida said warmly. 'I've just missed a bus and it's ages till the next one.'

They made their way through the crowd to the car park behind the shopping complex. She threw her packages on to the back seat of his car and settled herself beside him with a little sigh of relief. 'It's so hot!' she said, lifting her thick curls from the nape of her neck with both hands.

'Don't complain,' he said lightly. 'It can't last!'

'It's been glorious,' she agreed. 'But I think everyone is longing for a little rain — just for a change!'

'I expect we shall have a deluge,' he said drily. 'Have you seen the sky to the north?' He indicated the ominous black clouds that were rolling up with surprising speed, still distant but threatening. 'Do you suppose we shall miss that little lot?'

'It looks as if we are in for a storm,' she said, surprised.

He nodded. 'It's due.' He turned on the ignition and let out the clutch and the open-topped sports car moved forward smoothly.

He drove well and confidently, capable hands on the wheel as he manoeuvred the car along the narrow streets. Very soon, they reached the outskirts of the town and he could take a little of his attention from the road and glance at the girl beside him. She seemed relaxed, serene, her hands lying loosely in her lap. She looked cool and lovely in the thin summer frock and his heart contracted. It was the first time that they had been alone for more than a month and Luke knew that he would need a tight rein on his emotions. They had been getting on very well lately. But one wrong word, one impulsive act, could destroy all the trust and liking that he had worked so hard to achieve.

Elfrida sensed his glance and her heart fluttered nervously. But he had been reassuringly casual in his attitude during the last few weeks and she told herself firmly that she no longer had any reason to feel ill at ease with him. He had been attracted to her but he was over it now. They were reaching a new understanding and she was glad of it. She liked him better than she could have thought possible, remembering the antagonism that had once existed between them.

She did not know if he had changed. What did she know of him, after all? But Giles and the twins and various others had commented on the change in Luke. He was settling down, it was said. There was talk that he and Annabel meant to make a match of it. Certainly he was still very attentive to the girl and no one could doubt that Annabel was in love with him. For her part, Elfrida thought them ill-suited and Annabel much too young, not only in years, for a man like Luke. But it was none of her business and she would be pleased if he could find happiness with the girl who was reputedly very like the Sybil he had loved and lost. Or so she told herself . . .

The change, if change there was in him, might well be due to the fact that he had fallen in love again. And Annabel was very pretty, very appealing. Not the kind of wife one would expect a man like Luke to choose but he knew his own business best, no doubt. And Elfrida resolutely ignored the little clutch of dismay about her heart.

He talked idly, impersonally, touching on a wide range of subjects. And Elfrida responded dutifully, wondering if he was really as indifferent as he seemed or if he sought refuge behind a cool and formal friendliness. Having disliked and resented his advances with all their implication of a desire that owed nothing to liking let alone loving, she perversely found herself hungering for the touch of his hand. She studied his handsome face as he talked and her eyes rested on his mobile mouth and there was an odd little pain deep down inside as she recalled the day when he had cradled her face with unexpectedly tender hands and kissed her in a way that had threatened to tear the heart from her breast.

He did not drive fast but it seemed to Elfrida that the car was eating up the miles too rapidly. Much too soon, they would reach the village and he would drop her off at Clare Cottage and continue on his way to the Manor — and she would have absolutely no excuse to detain him, to keep him with her.

'Could we stop?' she said abruptly. 'I . . . I feel a little sick.' It was true. There was a strange and heavy sickness at the pit of her stomach but it was not travel sickness, she knew. For some inexplicable reason she was filled with a longing to be in his arms, to be held against his heart, to know the touch of his lips on her own, to see a certain smile in his eyes that was just for her, tender and reassuring, heartwarming. He might have many, many faults but she could not help wanting him with all her heart.

It had taken her too long to discover why she could not look forward to a lifetime with Giles. But now she knew that a moment of magic had swept her into loving Luke. She was as weak, as helpless before his magnetism as all those other women, she thought unhappily.

Luke stopped the car at the earliest opportunity, drawing in to the side of the country road. He turned to Elfrida, concerned. She did not look at all well, he thought, mistaking shock and dismay for illness. 'Did you have any lunch?' he demanded, a little stern, knowing that women were prone to miss out on a midday meal when other things occupied their minds. Shopping, for instance . . .

She shook her head. 'Everywhere was so crowded,' she said lamely.

'Silly girl.' His tone was gentle, indulgent. He opened the glove compartment and took out a hip flask. 'Some brandy will make you feel better, perhaps.'

'Oh no! Not on an empty stomach,' she said hastily. He looked doubtful. 'I don't want it,' she insisted. 'I shall be fine in a moment.'

'I ought to get you home.' He felt anxious, deeply protective towards her and was thankful to see that her colour was returning and her slender hands gripped each other less fiercely.

'You're really worried,' she said slowly, wonderingly.

'Well, of course,' he said, a little brusquely. 'Giles would have something to say to me if I didn't look after you in his absence!'

'You are frightened to death of Giles,' she scoffed gently. She looked at him with a tremulous little smile. 'You're a care-for-nobody, Luke ... everyone says so!'

A wry smile flickered about his lips. 'Then it must be true. Who am I to argue with everyone?' he drawled. 'Nevertheless, I don't care to offend my little brother these days. He is up in arms at the slightest criticism of you.'

She felt a slight pang at the words. 'Still criticizing me, Luke?' she asked with an admirable attempt at lightness. 'I thought you were reconciled to my friendship with Giles.'

'Oh, I am,' he said smoothly. 'You are good for him. He has matured since he met you ... and he doesn't take life quite so seriously.'

'You have changed your tune,' she said in surprise. 'A few weeks ago you were telling me to give him up!'

'Very high-handed of me,' he returned lightly. 'But I didn't know you so well then.'

'And now you approve,' she said with a bleak look in her eyes. He *was* indifferent. She might marry Giles with his blessing . . . and she might just as well! There was no future in loving this man to whom she had been just a fleeting fancy like all the others . . .

'Very much,' he said. He turned his head to smile at her and touched the back of his long fingers to her cheek in a careless caress. 'I've grown to like you very well.' The words were an understatement. He liked her, certainly. But the liking and admiration and respect that he felt were only a small part of the loving she had inspired.

He had never supposed that he could love again. Sybil had been everything to him. He had not known any real happiness or joy in living since her death. Nothing had really mattered and there had been no woman who could stir him to anything more than a casual sensuality. Then Elfrida had swept into his life without warning, as unlike Sybil as any woman could be and without a single good word for him. He had not expected to fall so deeply in love. He had not even recognized his need of her as loving for some time.

He wanted her with a desperate yearning. But there was tenderness and concern and the desire to protect and cherish and spend the rest of his life with her — all mixed up with the fierce sexual need that she evoked. No woman since Sybil had stirred him to such depths of emotion. He loved as only a man of strong passions can love and he had known for several days that he wanted to marry her. The man who had supposed that he valued his freedom above almost everything else in life had discovered that the thought of anything less than marriage where Elfrida was concerned was quite offensive to him.

He wished to marry her but he did not mean to rush his fences. He had broken down a great deal of the antagonism that she felt towards him. But she was a very long way from loving him. It was important to win her confidence before he grew anxious about winning her heart, he told himself firmly. Affection and trust were essential ingredients of any relationship between a man and a woman. She gave both to Giles without hesitation because Giles was a very different man to himself. Fortunately for his peace of mind, Luke knew instinctively that she was even further from loving Giles. So he could refer lightly to their friendship and play down his own feelings as he touched her soft cheek in a little gesture of affection which could not alarm her.

Elfrida was not alarmed. She was dismayed. Her heart welled with sudden sadness. But she would die rather than have him know how he hurt with those careless words, that meaningless touch, she thought with fierce pride.

'I'm glad,' she said brightly and the smile in her voice did not touch her eyes. 'Then you won't object to having me in the family?'

Abruptly she had made up her mind. Giles had been talking of marriage for weeks without actually pinning her down to a yes or no. Now she decided to marry him. Why not? He loved her and it was only sensible to accept that there was never going to be any happiness for her with his brother. She had left it too late to know that she loved him, she thought wryly, recalling the advances that she had rejected so firmly and with a finality that he had eventually accepted. But would encouragement have led to lasting happiness? Probably she would have been taken and forgotten like all the others, she thought unhappily — and that hurt too much even to contemplate!

Luke glanced at her swiftly, his jaw

tightening. 'Giles has actually proposed?' he asked, knowing it had been inevitable. What shook him was the implication in her words that she had agreed to marry his brother!

'And I accepted him,' Elfrida lied, a hint of challenge in her tawny eyes.

A nerve jumped in his jaw. 'You should have told me,' he said, very tense.

'I just did,' she said lightly, too concerned with her own pain to recognize the note of dismay in his voice. And now I have to tell Giles, she thought bleakly — and did not doubt his delight. 'You can't be surprised, Luke,' she swept on, forcing a smile. 'We haven't exactly hidden the way we feel about each other.'

He had not taken it seriously. He had never really looked on his brother as a serious rival. He had never really believed that she could be indifferent to him. He had been so sure that the flame burned as brightly for her as for himself but that, woman-like, she was merely taking her time to admit it. Now, too late, he realized that he had hidden his feeling for her too well.

The first heavy drops of rain began to fall. They had failed to notice the black clouds sweeping up to obscure the sun.

Luke said, a little abruptly: 'I must get you home.' He set the car in motion. He did not trust himself just then. He wanted to sweep her into his arms and pour out his love and beg her not to marry Giles. He had no pride any more. He needed her too much. But he loved her too much to embarrass her in such a way. After all, despite all his doubts, she cared for Giles and meant to be happy with him. He had been too blind, too sure of himself, to heed the truth.

'Yes,' Elfrida said quietly. 'I feel better now.' But in truth she felt very much worse. Sick dread had given way to agonizing certainty. It hurt to love a man who cared so little. It hurt to know that he would see her married to his brother without raising a finger to prevent it. It hurt to realize with such clarity that his interest in her had never been more than a fleeting physical attraction, soon forgotten.

She forced herself to smile, to thank him for bringing her home as she rescued her parcels from the back seat of the car.

'Will you come in?' she asked brightly.

Luke refused, as she had known that he would. He might say that he liked her; he might behave towards her with pleasant and reassuring friendliness; but in her heart Elfrida knew that he had not really forgiven her for rejecting him. He was a proud man and women did not usually say to him nay. And if they did it seemed that he did not give them a second chance!

12

Luke went away for a few days as soon as the engagement was announced. But as he had been talking for some time of a trip to town to attend to some neglected business, no one connected the two incidents.

When he returned, he had come to terms with the situation. He would always love Elfrida but there was no sin in loving that was not expressed by word or deed. He was a mature man and a promise of happiness was not always fulfilled. Disappointments were inevitable in life and could only be accepted with outward composure.

He would never marry now, he knew. But he had lived with that kind of resignation since Sybil's death and he could face the prospect of an emptiness in his life. It came a little harder because he was older and a second chance of happiness was more valuable than the first.

Sybil had been very much a part of his life. Elfrida had brought a new dimension to living. Sybil had died tragically and the memory of her was still poignant. Elfrida was very much alive, very lovely, very appealing . . . and he would have to spend the rest of his life with the constant reminder of her happiness with another man — and that man his own brother!

It was a very difficult situation. But he came back to Frisby with the knowledge that he had to live with it. And he was determined not to make things difficult for Giles or Elfrida . . .

Elfrida wore the huge diamond ring on her finger and gave an excellent impression of a happily-engaged young woman who looked forward to marrying the man she loved. She had accepted the inevitable but her heart was very heavy. She knew that Giles would do his best to make her happy and he could give her everything that any woman could want. It was just foolishness to feel so certain that she could never love him. In time she must be free of the stupid hunger for Luke's touch, Luke's kiss, Luke's embrace — and in time she must surely be able to love Giles as he deserved.

The wedding was arranged to take place in six weeks' time . . . just long enough for all the arrangements to be completed. They were to be married in the village church of St Peter's, very quietly. To please Giles, she had asked Annabel to be her bridesmaid. She knew it was inevitable that Giles should ask Luke to act as best man. Everyone speculated how long it would be before there was another wedding in the Inskip family.

Owen was delighted. He liked and approved his daughter's choice and it eased his mind to know that she would be happy and settled. He had decided to stay on at Clare Cottage, indefinitely. The new book had been well received by the publishers and Owen gave some of the credit to the peace and prettiness of his surroundings. He was getting older and he had seen much of the world and he did not want to be too far from his only child. Elfrida agreed with a little indulgent amusement in her eyes, knowing that he would be up and away as soon as the mood took him but pleased that he wished to remain in Frisby for some little while yet. She loved him dearly and she would miss him very much. She would miss their wanderings, too . . . so much part of her life for so long that she could not help wondering if she would be content with the quietness of Frisby. Or was it the quiet, unexciting steadiness of Giles that faintly disturbed her? He was a dear but he was just a little dull if one compared him to the challenge of Luke who could set a woman's pulses racing with one glance, one smile with all its enchantment.

Fortunately she did not see too much of Luke . . . and a woman who was about to marry one man ought not to be comparing him with another, she told herself firmly.

The days passed much too quickly. They were busy days. The hustle and bustle of wedding preparations satisfied some need within her and kept her from thinking too much about the step she was taking. After the wedding, they would honeymoon in Italy and return to live in the house that was being renovated and redecorated by a team of workmen. Inskip Lodge was only a stone's throw from the Manor but at least they would not be living under the same roof with Luke, Elfrida was thankful to learn.

The Duncans would also be near neighbours. Elfrida liked them both. The Colonel and his wife were fond of Giles and she guessed that they had hoped that he and Annabel might make a match of it. But they did not allow their disappointment to show.

One evening, dining at the Hall, she idly wondered why he and Annabel had not made a match of it. Seeing them with their heads together, oblivious to everyone else in the room, she knew that they shared a rapport that excluded her all unconsciously. They had a special feeling for each other that she supposed she ought to mind. But she felt guilty rather than jealous. If she had not come to Frisby with Owen and struck up a friendship with Giles, he might have loved Annabel rather than herself and pleased both families and all their friends by marrying her. And Annabel would not have been so silly as to encourage Luke's attentions, perhaps . . . or Giles would have stepped in before they could have gone to her head.

It was difficult to know how matters stood between Luke and Annabel. Were they having an affair? Or was he merely indulging her in a little flirtation to take her mind off Giles' desertion? She could not imagine Luke having such a disinterested motive for his pursuit of a very pretty girl! And had Annabel really been swept off her feet by the very attractive Luke or was she merely seeking some consolation for the loss of Giles?

She had declared delight at the engagement and congratulated them warmly and shown pleasure at the prospect of being a bridesmaid. But Elfrida did not think that she was truly pleased by Giles' plans to marry someone else. It seemed that they had always been very close and it was possible that Annabel had cherished a dream of becoming his wife one day . . .

In fact, Annabel had never dreamed of marrying Giles. He had always been not quite a brother and more than a friend . . . he had always been just Giles. Not one of her flirts for he would only laugh if she tried to set her cap at him. But dear . . . dearer than anyone else she knew. Closer than anyone else could ever be, she thought at times. He understood her so well. They spoke the same language . . . it was as simple as that!

Luke was handsome, fascinating,

exciting — and it was a dream come true to be noticed by him. But some dreams were best left unfulfilled, she had discovered. She was not always at her ease with Luke. He was so much older, so much more experienced — and she felt a child when he smiled at her with something very like indulgence rather than desire in his grey eyes.

Sometimes, when they were together, he seemed a million miles away and she felt herself to be the last person in the world that he wished to be with. Sometimes, when they kissed, she felt that he was a stranger and she wondered what on earth she was doing in his arms. Sometimes, when she was alone and looking very carefully into her heart, she doubted that she loved him at all and wondered if it would be a relief when he slipped away to the arms of someone else as he inevitably would. She did not believe that he cared for her and she wondered what he gained from their casual relationship.

It was a relief to turn to Giles. She could relax and be herself and say whatever came into her head and not wonder if he was bored with her chatter or regarded her with little more than amused tolerance. She knew that Giles liked to be with her. They had so much in common. They understood each other so well. Giles was very, very dear to her. Giles was reassuringly the same day in and day out, unlike his moody brother. Giles was . . . oh, just Giles and she simply could not imagine her life without him!

She listened with real interest and a glow of admiration to his account of a minor contretemps with an employee at the Home Farm, very sure that he had handled the business better than anyone else could possibly have done. He was scrupulously fair and swift to see both sides of any argument. There was no one like Giles, she thought on a sudden surge of affection . . . and she smiled on him with tender, loving warmth.

Giles' heart turned over with the sudden realization that he loved her, had always loved her, could never truly love anyone else. 'Oh, Anna!' he said tensely, gripping her slim hand on a sudden wave of emotion. 'This is a mess!'

She nodded, knowing what was in his mind. She knew that he felt as she did that they were right for each other as no one else could possibly be right for either of them. 'Yes,' she said, smiling reassuringly into his anxious eyes. 'But you'll put it right, Giles.'

Her confidence in him soothed the fierce agitation of his heart. 'I must,' he said firmly . . .

He deserved to be hung, drawn and quartered for doing such a thing to a lovely girl like Elfrida. He did not know how he could have been so blind, so stupid. A ridiculous infatuation had caused him to briefly lose sight of the fact that he had made up his mind to marry Annabel when she was still in her cradle and the resolution had strengthened with the years. It was unthinkable that he could spend his life with anyone else!

He was deeply thankful that there was time to cancel the wedding. Another week or so and he would have been a married man and he would have found it extremely difficult to declare that it was all a mistake!

It said much for his strength of character that he did not shrink from the difficult task of breaking the news to Elfrida. He did not even wait for the dawn of a new day. He chafed throughout the remainder of the evening until it was time to take her home — and as soon as they had driven through the gates of the Hall, he took a deep breath and said quietly: 'I've something to tell you.'

She looked at him quickly. 'That sounds ominous.' She spoke lightly but the little leap of her heart responded to a certain resolution in his tone.

'Yes. It isn't easy for me and it isn't pleasant for you — and I hope you'll hate me for it. Because I shall feel terrible if you go on caring for me when I don't deserve it. Elfrida, I can't marry you!' The last words came in a little rush.

She was flooded with relief. She wanted to laugh and sing and exclaim with delight at her reprieve. Her heart had been declaring for days that she ought not to marry him, that it was wrong and foolish, that he deserved better than a reluctant bride. 'It's Annabel, isn't it?' she said, almost joyfully.

'You knew!'

'I don't think anyone can look at you both and not know,' she told him, smiling.

He was astonished that she was taking it so well. At the same time, he hoped that it was not simply reaction to a shock that would show itself in more frightening force when he was not around to comfort and reassure her. It must be a terrible blow to her — to any girl so near to her wedding day! How could she smile and seem so relaxed and refer to the rapport between himself and Annabel with so little apparent anguish!

'I've treated you abominably,' he said unhappily.

'You've been wonderful to me ever since we met,' she refuted firmly.

He reached swiftly for her hand. 'I'm very fond of you,' he said quietly.

She lifted his hand to her cheek in a little gesture of affection. 'Dear Giles . . . I'm very fond of you, too. But you haven't broken my heart. I thought we could build a successful marriage on friendship and affection and common interests . . . and I daresay we could have done so if Annabel didn't exist.' Or Luke, she added silently, her heart contracting with the thought of him.

'I think you are trying to spare me,' Giles said wryly.

She shook her head. 'No . . . truly! I don't think I could have married you next week even believing that you loved me. It wouldn't have been the right thing to do. Marriage is such an important step. I don't think I realized what a commitment it is until we went through the service with the vicar last night. I think I knew then that I couldn't do it. But it might have taken several days to muster the courage to tell you so!'

'What will you do?' he asked anxiously.

She understood him. The whole district would be buzzing with speculation and it would not be very pleasant for her to endure the glances and the whispers. For some unaccountable reason, public sympathy was always with the bride if a wedding was called off at almost the last moment. No one ever believed that she might have realized her mistake in time. It was always assumed that the man had made good his escape, leaving his bride with a broken heart. But this bride had a thankful heart. For marriage to Giles or anyone else was not the answer to her problem.

'Oh, I shall go away,' she decided. 'I think it will be better for everyone . . . including Annabel. I expect Owen will stay till the end of the summer. He is very happy in Frisby. But I shall go to stay with friends. You mustn't worry about me, Giles. I shall be fine.'

'I wish you didn't have to go,' he said ruefully. 'I shall miss you . . . we all will! You have become a very dear friend, Elfrida.'

She smiled at him with affectionate warmth and promised to return, to keep in touch. But in her heart she knew that she must put the village behind her for ever — Frisby and the Inskips. And particularly Luke whom she loved. She knew intuitively that he would tug at her heart for the rest of her life. There was no rhyme nor reason in the way she felt about him and she was not the first woman to love him, to ache for him, to realize the futility of her feeling for him. For it seemed that Luke was a man who could only love once in a lifetime and his heart had been buried with the girl who should have been his bride . . .

The next morning, Elfrida drove down the village street, looking about her for the last time. She felt a pang as she passed the houses, the little shops, the school and the church where she and Giles might have been married. It was better this way, she told herself firmly. But Frisby had begun to feel like home to the girl who had suffered so much from her father's wanderlust. Strangely, Owen also loved the quiet village and did not wish to leave it. Perhaps he was growing old. Or perhaps it was what he had been seeking all his life. But he was saddened by the thought of packing up and moving on when he had been contemplating the possibility of buying Clare Cottage. However, he had assured Elfrida that he would close up the cottage and follow her to town very shortly.

He had not attempted to prevent her from rushing away . . . or running away if one chose to regard it in that light. She *was* running away, of course. Not from the disappointment of her cancelled wedding. Not from public speculation and sympathy. But from a man who did not care if she married his brother or not because his own interest in her had died an abrupt death.

There was no future in caring for Luke. So she would go away, very far from Frisby and all its poignant memories, and do her best to forget a foolish love that had been born of a moment of magic . . .

13

Luke hammered on the cottage door, convinced that Elfrida was simply not answering to his knock. He could not blame her if she wished to have nothing more to do with any member of his family. At the same time, he wanted to see her, to talk to her, to discover for himself how deeply she was affected by Giles' unexpected turnabout.

He had been shocked, incredulous. He knew that there had always been a close understanding between Giles and Annabel but he had dismissed it as boy-and-girl sentimentality. It had not occurred to him that they might wish to marry . . . and he had not thought it possible that Giles could snatch at happiness at the expense of someone else's heartbreak. Of course Giles declared that Elfrida's heart was not broken . . . it was exactly what a proud

214

girl like Elfrida would claim and exactly what his conscience-stricken brother would wish to believe!

Elfrida was very much in love with Giles. He had seen the glow in her tawny eyes when she looked at him, had heard the smile in her voice when she spoke of him. He had observed the pride and happiness and elation of the weeks spent in wedding preparations and noticed how often she fingered the heavy ring that Giles had given to her to mark their engagement. She had shown all the signs of loving, of looking forward to a life spent with his brother.

And Giles said with evident relief in eyes and voice that she had mistaken her feelings just as he had, that she had never really loved him and that she had meant to call off the wedding if he had not done so! Giles was a fool! Giles was so thankful to have escaped so lightly from a morass of his own making that he would not doubt or question anything that Elfrida said to him.

His heart was wrenched with concern

for the woman he loved. He knew all that she must be going through . . . so much worse to be jilted than bereaved, so much worse for a woman who knew hopes and dreams that seldom entered a man's head or heart. A woman gave herself completely to loving. A man kept something of himself in reserve.

Luke had driven at speed down the country lanes to reach the cottage, knowing the fierce desire to comfort the girl who had suffered at his brother's hands . . . and now he hammered at the door.

It was opened at last by Owen. 'My dear fellow!' he expostulated angrily at sight of the caller.

'Is Elfrida here? I must see her,' Luke declared without ceremony.

Owen looked at him without liking. He was deeply troubled by the sadness he had sensed in his daughter. 'She isn't here,' he said firmly. 'She left this morning . . . and she isn't coming back. Do you blame her? I'm very angry with that brother of yours, Inskip. He has treated my girl very badly.'

'Yes, I know. I'm very angry with him, too,' Luke said brusquely. 'Where is Elfrida? You must know.'

'Certainly I know!' Owen said testily. 'But there's no point in chasing up to town. She won't want to see any of you!'

'I think she'll see me,' Luke said with a confidence he did not feel.

'Hmmph! Liked you less than your brothers,' Owen said bluntly. 'Always arguing, weren't you? Write to her, young man. I'll see that she gets your letter. Then if she wants to see you she'll get in touch.' He closed the door with an air of finality. Believing that he was protecting Elfrida from further pain, he went back to his books. She was a sensible girl and much too proud to let a young whippersnapper break her heart and he did not doubt that there would be a succession of young men to take her mind off her disappointment. She would get over the beastly business much sooner without reminders of the might-have-been.

Luke glowered at the heavy wooden door. Then he turned on his heel and strode to his car. He recognized obstinacy when he saw it and it was obvious that Owen Hendry did not mean to be co-operative. The suggestion that he should write to Elfrida did not appeal to him. The kind of things he wanted to say to her were not easily expressed in a letter, he thought wryly. He would have to find her by other means. But it might be as difficult as finding a needle in a haystack . . .

Elfrida went to friends in Knightsbridge and stayed with them while she hunted for a flat and waited for Owen to join her in town. She talked to him on the telephone and found him in the throes of re-writing a chapter of the new book at the request of the publishers. He had decided to remain at the cottage for the time being and Elfrida was to enjoy herself with her friends and not worry about him or anything else.

He did not mention Luke's visit because he had forgotten it. There had been no letter for him to forward and he assumed that the Inskips were forgetting Elfrida as rapidly as he hoped that she was forgetting them.

The social whirl of life in town was a far cry from the quiet peace of Frisby. Elfrida had scarcely a moment to fret over her broken engagement even if she had been inclined to do so. But all the gaiety in the world could not have eased the persistent ache about her heart. It was foolish but she looked for Luke wherever she went . . . and sometimes she fancied that she saw him. Walking along a pavement on the other side of the road, disappearing down the metal-tipped steps of an underground station, seated in the far corner of a restaurant, briefly glimpsed in a crowded theatre vestibule. Her heart and mind and eyes played the most ridiculous tricks on her, she thought wearily, disappointed yet again as a tall man with auburn hair that gleamed gold in the bright lights turned and proved to be a stranger, after all.

Luke Inskip was not the only man in the world with hair of that particular colour and grey eyes that crinkled when he smiled and the kind of physical magnetism that caused women's heads to turn. But it seemed that he was the only man who could mean anything to her. She did not lack escorts, admirers, even lovers if she had wanted them. She could enjoy an evening in the company of an attractive man, to some extent. But there was no magic, no enchantment, no excitement in the touch of another man's hand, the pressure of his lips on her own, the warmth of his arms about her slender body. Only one man had the power to fill her heart with dreams and her mind with memories of magic moments that she would never know again.

She yearned for Luke and knew she might never see him again. He was constantly in her thoughts, always in her heart — and it did not help to tell herself to stop loving him, wanting him, dreaming impossible dreams of living her life with him. She told herself that if Luke had still felt the smallest flicker of interest or attraction or desire he would have sought her out as soon as he learned that she was not to be his sister-in-law, after all. It had been foolish to entertain the hope that he had been held back by love for his brother and concern for Giles' happiness. She was free now and he knew it — and did nothing.

It was very hot and airless in London during that month of August. Elfrida thought with longing of the country with its green fields and shady copses and quiet river walks. She was terribly tempted to drive down to Frisby, ostensibly to visit her father but in reality with the hope of encountering Luke, however briefly and however frustratingly. But she resisted temptation.

After a tiring morning of looking at

particularly unsuitable flats at exorbitant prices, Elfrida made her way to the London Hilton to keep an appointment with a friend.

She was a few minutes early and expected the unpunctual Susie to be late so she settled herself in a comfortable seat in the foyer with a magazine. Every now and again she glanced towards the swing doors, expecting her friend.

A tall, lean man in a silver grey suit with matching shirt and tie pushed his way into the foyer. Elfrida glanced at him and away again, chiding her heart for leaping so foolishly. She had already discovered that there were a million men with similar colouring and looks and physique to the man she loved. She returned to her magazine, wondering a little bleakly why only Luke could make her weak with wanting. Why was it so impossible for her to love any other man? What was it about Luke Inskip that set him apart from other men? His wildness, his careless pursuit of women, his utter disregard for anything in life but his own desires? She ought not to love such a man! But she did . . .

Luke's glance swept over the large and luxurious vestibule with its comfortable seats and the bustle of comings and goings . . . it was a popular meeting place for friends as well as a very successful hotel that catered for the needs of many foreign visitors. Luke was staying at the hotel for a few days. He had come to town in the hope of finding Elfrida. Surprisingly, Giles seemed to know nothing of her town friends. Theirs had been planned as a quiet wedding and few people had been invited. Yet she must have many friends in and around London. He had decided to look up some of his own friends in town who might move in the same circle as the Hendrys.

He went to the desk for his key and then to the kiosk for a newspaper. Turning towards the busy lifts, his attention was caught by the entrance of a girl in green velvet trousers and blouson, a matching cloak swinging from her shoulders, her fair hair cut very short in a silken cap that enhanced the gamine prettiness of her looks. She was striking and it was not only Luke's head that turned. He smiled faintly, amused by a flamboyance that was obviously out to attract attention. Then he stiffened. For a slender young woman in an elegant white suit, black hair plaited into a gleaming knob on the nape of her neck, rose from one of the couches and moved forward to greet the newcomer. It was unmistakably Elfrida. He knew it even before she turned her face slightly as the two girls kissed cheeks in greeting.

His heart was pounding heavily. Another moment and he would have entered the waiting lift and never known how near he was to his love. He took an impulsive step towards her, his lips framing her name . . . and then he paused, as unsure of himself as an inexperienced boy in the presence of the girl he loved. How would she welcome his unexpected presence in town? And would she welcome him at all when he might be a very painful reminder of much that she wished to forget?

While he hesitated, Elfrida talked to her friend, wholly unaware of him. Susie explained her lateness with laughing insouciance. She was rehearsing a new play that opened the next night and last-minute problems had made it difficult for her to get away. 'I must be back by two,' she warned. 'So keep an eye on the time for me. You know how I rattle on. Darling, there's a gorgeous man heading this way. I hope he's a friend. Are you expecting anyone to join us?'

Elfrida turned. 'No one,' she said lightly . . . and then her heart seemed to stop as she met Luke's smiling eyes.

He tried to appear casual, as though it was the likeliest thing in the world that they should encounter each other in a hotel vestibule so many miles and a different world from the quiet village

225

where they had first met. 'London is a small place, after all,' he said lightly, smiling, taking her hand.

Elfrida stared at him, eyes widening in disbelief and delight. All the colour fled from her lovely face with the shock of seeing him. 'It *was* you . . . ' she said foolishly.

She had dismissed the fancy that it was Luke who entered the hotel through its swing doors. It could not be him for all her hoping. Yet here he was, smiling down at her, clasping her hand — and the very real warmth in his grey eyes set her heart racing so that she could scarcely breathe. She could only look at him and think how much she had missed him and how dear he was — and she did not care that he might see in her eyes and hear in her voice all the loving and longing that filled her heart.

'How are you?' he asked gently, noting the pallour and the faint shadows beneath the lovely eyes. His heart contracted with concern. She had suffered . . . and he almost knew hatred for the brother who had caused her pain and bitter disappointment.

Elfrida pulled herself together and gently withdrew her hand. 'I'm fine,' she said lightly. 'What are you doing in town?' She was very conscious of the curious Susie, looking from one to the other with a knowing little smile in her eyes. 'Oh, I'm sorry . . . Susie Brent — Luke Inskip. He . . . he lives in the village where we had a cottage while Owen was writing the latest book,' she said, a little flurried. 'Lord of the Manor, in fact — aren't you, Luke?' Her tone was light, teasing, just a little self-conscious.

'How fascinating!' Susie fluttered her long lashes in instinctive coquetry and allowed her hand to rest in his clasp. 'I've always wanted to meet a country gentleman.'

'Elfrida will tell you that I'm no gentleman,' he returned, smiling at his love in a way that was meant to remind her of their early encounters. She coloured faintly and smiled but he noticed that she did not meet his eyes. He knew a pang of disappointment. So much hope had leaped in his heart at that first betrayal of her pleasure in their meeting. But perhaps she was only anxious for news of Giles, he warned himself wryly.

'Even better,' Susie said outrageously, laughing up at him. 'Elfrida and I are about to have some lunch . . . why don't you join us? I'm longing to tell you all about myself.'

He looked to Elfrida to second the careless invitation. She said uncertainly: 'Oh, I expect you have other plans . . . '

'No,' he said firmly, refusing to be dismissed. 'I shall be delighted if you will allow me to take you both to lunch — and I shall certainly be the most envied man in town!'

It was not the most enjoyable hour of Elfrida's life. She knew that she was a little stiff and much too quiet while Susie flirted gaily with Luke as she did with every man she met — and it seemed to Elfrida that Luke responded as he did to every lovely woman who came in his way. She could not help wondering despondently if he had approached her only because he wanted an introduction to Susie who drew the men like a magnet. He certainly encouraged her to talk at length about herself and her success in show business. He was very attentive, Elfrida thought, trying not to show that she minded. Susie was attractive, of course . . . and she had a personality to match her looks and vitality. She was just the kind of woman that Luke would find interesting.

Susie snatched a moment when he was busy with the wine waiter to whisper: 'Is he the man you were going to marry?'

Elfrida swiftly regretted the impulse to confide in her friend. She shook her head. 'His brother,' she said briefly.

'Well, if he's anything like this one then you were mad to let him slip through your fingers,' Susie declared in her usual blunt fashion. 'He's really something! Bring him to the party tomorrow night!'

A little later, she rose reluctantly with the announcement that she must get back to rehearsals. Elfrida's heart plunged at the thought of being on her own with Luke. It was what she wanted but she was suddenly consumed with a painful shyness and the terrible fear that she would blurt out her love for him and make a fool of herself.

They left the Hilton together and emerged into the bright sunshine of Park Lane. Susie scrambled into a taxi which departed with her waving from the open window and shouting noisy farewells. Elfrida was a little relieved when the taxi turned a corner and her extrovert friend ceased to attract so much attention.

She stood on the pavement outside the hotel, regarding Luke a little uncertainly, wondering if the moment had come for them to bid each other goodbye and go their separate ways or whether he would take the opportunity to spend some time alone with her . . .

14

Elfrida hitched her bag further on to her shoulder. Luke turned swiftly, fancying the movement implied departure. 'You aren't leaving me, I hope,' he said abruptly, a sudden intensity in his grey eyes. She could walk away and he wouldn't know how to find her again, he thought wryly. He knew that she had been constrained by her friend's presence. He hoped against hope that dislike of him had not been another reason for her coolness.

'Well, I do have a hair appointment,' Elfrida said briskly. But her heart lifted at his apparent desire to keep her by his side and she added hastily: 'At three-thirty.'

'Then you can spare me an hour,' Luke said in a tone that brooked no argument. He took her elbow in a firm clasp. 'It's a lovely day. Let's walk in the park.' He guided her through the maze of traffic to the other side of the busy road and into Hyde Park with its pleasant greenery and tall trees and quiet paths where lovers strolled in the sunshine. Very soon, the roar of traffic receded in the distance as they walked towards the Serpentine. Luke took her hand and tucked it into his arm and covered it with his own, keeping her close to his side. He looked down at her with a little smile in his eyes.

It was a dream, Elfrida decided. There was an unreality about this walk in a London park with the man she loved. And because it was all a dream she could allow herself to believe the warm tenderness in his grey eyes, the reassurance in that faintly possessive clasp of his hand, the promise in his smile. Her heart swelled with the happiness that could only come from a feeling of being loved by the only one in all the world who mattered.

'How have you been?' Luke asked quietly.

'Fine — I told you.' His question had shattered the dream. She faltered a little before the look in his eyes. 'How is Giles? And Annabel? Have they fixed a date? Or are they married already'?

'Not yet. They are both well.' He was a little brusque to cover his concern for her pain. He admired the courage which enabled her to speak so lightly of the couple who had hurt her so much.

Elfrida was troubled by his tone. Did it hurt him to talk of Annabel's wish to marry his brother? Had he cared more than anyone had suspected? Had all his hopes of happiness been dashed a second time? 'I'm sorry,' she said impulsively. 'That was tactless. When you didn't mention ... I mean, I should have realized — I'm sorry, Luke,' she said again, floundering.

'Sorry? For me?' he said in astonishment.

He was proud, she reminded herself, wishing she had not spoken of Giles and Annabel. But it would have seemed so odd to avoid their names altogether

— and she did not want him to suppose that she was too hurt to talk about them. She did not want him to imagine that Giles had broken her heart! 'You are fond of Annabel,' she said gently. 'But she wouldn't be a good wife for you, Luke.'

'I never had any thought of marrying her,' he said bluntly. 'What put that idea into your head?'

'Oh . . . people talk,' she stumbled.

He looked down at her, eyes narrowing. 'Too damn much!' he said impatiently.

She nodded, flooded with relief. So he was not in love with Annabel, had never even thought of loving her! It did not bring him any nearer to loving her, Elfrida cautioned herself, but at least he still had a heart to give — unless he had truly buried it with Sybil. 'I ought to have remembered what you told me,' she said, striving for lightness. 'That you aren't a marrying man.'

'I'm not,' he said abruptly. 'It takes a rare woman to make me change my mind . . . and it certainly isn't Annabel.'

'I'm glad,' she said warmly. 'You and Giles have always been so close. I was sorry to think that she might be the cause of a rift between you.'

'There was the beginnings of a rift,' he admitted wryly. 'But it's healed . . . and it had nothing to do with Annabel. You were responsible for that, Elfrida.'

'Me?' she echoed in surprise and dismay.

'You couldn't expect me to feel well-disposed towards a brother who was planning to marry the woman I wanted,' he said quietly.

Her heart stood still. But her more cautious head considered his words. She had known that he wanted her. He had not made it a secret in the early days. But his kind of wanting had nothing to do with loving . . . and it was his love she wanted so desperately.

'But you made it clear that you didn't want me,' he went on, a little harsh. 'So all my best-laid plans for taking you away from Giles came to nothing. But you see how ready I was to take my happiness at the expense of his, Elfrida. That's the kind of man I am. That's why you love Giles who is a very different man to me.'

'I don't love Giles,' she said, her heart hammering.

He stopped abruptly. 'You promised to marry him!' he exclaimed, almost angry.

'He never proposed,' she said truthfully. 'I told you that he had but I lied. I asked Giles to marry me — more or less! Manoeuvred him, if you like.' She shrugged.

'Why? What was the point in that?' he demanded impatiently, realizing how much time had been wasted. He could have reached for the happiness that only she could give if he had not been so fearful of coming between her and Giles. Yet Giles had never wanted anyone but Annabel. And Elfrida . . . what did Elfrida want, he wondered wryly. He searched her tawny eyes almost desperately for the smallest evidence that she wanted him.

'I don't know. I suppose there wasn't any point,' she said honestly. 'I didn't really want Giles. But I was so miserable and he was there . . . like you and yet not like you,' she added in unconscious betrayal. 'I thought we might be happy together.'

'You gave a convincing display of wanting him,' Luke said, a little tense, scarcely daring to believe the implication of her words.

She smiled. 'I was out to convince you,' she said, suddenly not caring if he knew that she loved him. There was no shame in loving. He had come to like her and might even be a little fond of her, she thought hopefully. Perhaps they could be friends and perhaps one day . . . one day!

Everything fell into place. She had been miserable because she loved him and doubted him — and heaven knew that she had sufficient cause to doubt, he thought with sudden regret for a way of life that had earned him a reputation for loving too lightly. He wondered what he could say or do to convince her that the love he offered was real and lasting — and decided that the simplest way must be the best.

'You took a hell of a risk,' he said slowly. 'Giles is a man of his word. He would have married you if you'd held him to it . . . but it seems that you called off the wedding. I thought Giles had let you down and it seemed so out of character. And I couldn't believe that you were the kind of girl to marry a man if you didn't love him.'

Elfrida looked beyond him at the gleaming water of the Serpentine, bright in the sun. Then she looked up at him with her heart in her eyes. 'There's loving and *loving*,' she said softly. 'But I couldn't marry Giles. I want you, Luke.'

'I want you, too,' he said with sudden urgency . . . and Elfrida knew that it did not matter that he said *want* instead of *love*. The glow in his grey eyes and the betraying tremor in his voice spoke of his feeling for her in a way that all the words in the world could not.

He reached to cradle her face within his two hands, infinitely gentle, and he kissed her with such loving tenderness that she was convinced that he felt just as she did. It was one more moment to treasure for ever. But this time she knew that it was only the beginning of a magic that would last a lifetime . . .

THE END

We do hope that you have enjoyed reading this large print book.

Did you know that all of our titles are available for purchase?

We publish a wide range of high quality large print books including:
Romances, Mysteries, Classics
General Fiction
Non Fiction and Westerns

Special interest titles available in large print are:
The Little Oxford Dictionary
Music Book, Song Book
Hymn Book, Service Book

Also available from us courtesy of Oxford University Press:
Young Readers' Dictionary
(large print edition)
Young Readers' Thesaurus
(large print edition)

For further information or a free brochure, please contact us at:
Ulverscroft Large Print Books Ltd.,
The Green, Bradgate Road, Anstey,
Leicester, LE7 7FU, England.
Tel: (00 44) **0116 236 4325**
Fax: (00 44) **0116 234 0205**

Other titles in the
Linford Romance Library:

CONVALESCENT HEART

Lynne Collins

They called Romily the Snow Queen, but once she had been all fire and passion, kindled into loving by a man's kiss and sure it would last a lifetime. She still believed it would, for her. It had lasted only a few months for the man who had stormed into her heart. After Greg, how could she trust any man again? So was it likely that surgeon Jake Conway could pierce the icy armour that the lovely ward sister had wrapped about her emotions?